Praise for the Bluford Series:

"The Bluford Series is mind-blowing!"
— *Adam A.*

"These books are *deep*. They show readers who are going through difficult problems that they are not alone in the world. And they even help teach you how to deal with situations in a positive way."
— *Vianny C.*

"I love all of the books in the Bluford Series. They are page-turners full of secrets, surprises, and lots of drama."
— *Kayli A.*

"Each Bluford book starts out with a bang. And then, when you turn the page, it gets even better!"
— *Alex M.*

"The Bluford Series is amazing! They make you feel like you're inside the story, like everything's happening to you."
— *Ricardo N.*

"These are life-changing stories that make you think long after you reach the last page."
— *Eddie M.*

"I found it very easy to lose myself in these books. They kept my interest from beginning to end and were always realistic. The characters are vivid, and the endings left me in eager anticipation of the next book."
— *Keziah J.*

"For the first time in high school, I read a book I liked. For real, the Bluford Series is *tight.*"

— *Jermaine B.*

"These are thrilling, suspenseful books filled with real-life scenarios that make them too good to put down."

—*DeAndria B.*

"My school is just like Bluford High. The characters are just like people I know. These books are *real!*"

— *Jessica K.*

"I have never been so interested in books in my entire life. I'm surprised how much the Bluford Series catches my attention. Once I start reading, I can't stop. I keep staying up into the midnight hours trying to finish."

— *Andrew C.*

"The Bluford Series are the best books I have ever read. They are like TVs in my head."

— *Yaovi C.*

"One of my friends told me how good the Bluford Series is. She was right. Once I started reading, I couldn't stop, not even to sleep!"

— *Bibi R.*

"I love the Bluford books and the stories they tell. They're so real and action-packed, I feel like I'm inside the pages, standing next to the characters!"

—*Michael D.*

Survivor

Paul Langan

Series Editor: Paul Langan

TOWNSEND PRESS
www.townsendpress.com

Books in the Bluford Series

Copyright © 2013 by Townsend Press, Inc.
Printed in the United States of America

9 8 7 6 5 4 3 2 1

Cover illustration © 2013 by Gerald Purnell

Townsend Press, Inc.
439 Kelley Drive
West Berlin, NJ 08091
permissions@townsendpress.com

ISBN: 978-1-59194-304-4

Library of Congress Control Number:
2012953524

For the 1 in 4 girls and 1 in 6 boys
who are survivors

Chapter 1

"Oh my God, Tarah! Check out this picture!" yelled Rochelle Barnes, Tarah Carson's twenty-year-old cousin. Rochelle sat on the rumpled lime green couch in Tarah's living room, leafing through an old photo book.

"Can we stop with the pictures already?" Tarah protestcd, eyeing the stack of old albums piled on the floor. Her cousin kept flipping the pages as if Tarah hadn't said a word.

"Look at this one!" Rochelle said with a cackle. "Your braids look crazy, girl. And look at all them beads! Remember how we used to wear 'em back in the day?"

"You wore braids too, Aunt Tarah?" asked Kayla, Rochelle's four-year-old daughter. Even though she and Tarah were cousins, Kayla had always called Tarah her aunt.

"That's right, Kayla. I wore 'em just like you," Tarah said, gently resting her hand on the little girl's shoulder. She didn't want Kayla to know that she hated looking at old pictures of herself, especially the ones Rochelle had grabbed.

"Here's another one," Rochelle said, pointing to a photograph. "See how much you and Aunt Tarah look alike, Kayla? You almost look like you could be sisters." The little girl smiled shyly and ate one of the grapes Tarah had given her as a snack.

Rochelle and Kayla lived with Tarah's aunt Lucille in a small stucco house a few blocks away. Nearly every weekend, usually Saturday mornings, Rochelle and Kayla walked over for a visit. Often, Rochelle would leave her daughter there for a few hours so she could get her shopping done. Tarah didn't mind. She loved playing with her little cousin or taking her to the park not far from Bluford High School, where Tarah would start eleventh grade in another month.

Looking at the stack of photo albums next to Rochelle, Tarah wished she could go for a walk right now. Anything to get away from the old pictures and the haunting memories they triggered.

"You gonna look through *all* of them right now? That's gonna take hours," Tarah complained.

"So? It's not like you're goin' some-where. School's out, and you don't work on Saturdays." Rochelle snapped the first album closed and grabbed a second one.

Tarah knew her cousin was right, but she also knew which pictures were inside the smudged maroon album with the split corners. It had been hidden in the back of the cluttered hall closet where Tarah buried it years ago. She felt an uncomfortable twinge in her stomach as Rochelle plopped it on her lap and flipped it open. It was a collection of photos she didn't want to see.

"I don't wanna spend the whole day looking at them old things," Tarah huffed. "Let's take Kayla for a walk. We can look at those later."

"No, go through them *now*," urged Tarah's mother, Clarice Carson, as she emerged from the bedroom and sat down heavily on the couch. Mom worked as a corrections officer and was one of the toughest women Tarah knew. "You been dragging your feet with this for months. I asked you to do this, like, five times already. The reunion for Aunt Deborah is in two weeks. She's my great-aunt, Tarah. My grandmother's sister. She's the only one from her generation we got left, and she's turning ninety. At this point, she don't want presents, but you know how she is about family. I figured we'd gather pictures of everybody and give them to her. She's gonna love 'em. But we need to get started on it *now*!" Mom insisted.

The twinge in Tarah's belly grew into a dull queasiness. Her stomach had actually been bothering her on and off for weeks, ever since her mother started pressuring her about the reunion. But it got worse this morning when Rochelle called to say she was coming over to look through the old photographs.

"Ooh, here's a good one," Rochelle chimed in, holding up the book so everyone could see. "It's got everyone from our side. Everybody looks good, too, except for you, Tar. You ain't smiling at all."

"Like you never took a bad picture, Rochelle," Tarah grumbled, uncomfortable with everyone staring at the old photo. "I seen a few of you smiling with them big ol' buck teeth you used to have, but you don't see me pointing it out to everyone."

"You mean like what you're doin' right now?" Rochelle snapped. "Why you gettin' so upset? I'm only saying what I see. Look." Rochelle held the photo album out to her.

"Can I see?" Kayla asked between bites of another grape.

Tarah didn't want anyone to look at the picture, let alone Kayla. She knew Rochelle's description of her face was right. She could still remember fragments of the day when the family gathered in Municipal Park to celebrate her aunt Linda's wedding. Relatives had come from all over to be there, and they would spend the sunny afternoon barbecuing and listening to music. Tarah knew it should have been fun, and for most people there, it was. She had heard them talking about it for years. But it was a day Tarah never mentioned—and tried hard to forget.

"Yeah, you don't look happy, Aunt Tarah," Kayla said, inspecting the photo.

"I had a stomachache that day," Tarah replied quickly, getting up from the table and heading to the kitchen so no one would see her face. Just being near the pictures made her feel edgy and uncomfortable all these years later.

"It's true. She did," Mom added, rubbing Kayla's back. "Couldn't get her to talk or smile at all that day. She spent the whole afternoon in the shade with Aunt Deborah. Good thing she was there, too, 'cause I couldn't keep my eyes on her with all them cousins runnin' around. It was like a circus that whole weekend. Gonna be like that again in two weeks. We're expecting over eighty people!"

"For real? Are you serious?" Rochelle exclaimed.

"Mmm hmm. Maybe more if people bring friends. That reminds me. Tarah, is Coop comin'? And what about Darcy and her sister?"

Tarah hadn't told her boyfriend, Cooper Hodden, about the party. In fact, she hadn't mentioned it to anyone. Normally, she loved cookouts and being with her friends. But this gathering was different. From the moment Mom first mentioned the guests that might come, Tarah felt uneasy. Those feelings had grown so strong that she had tried to block the whole event from her mind.

"Yeah, I guess they're coming," Tarah answered.

"You *guess*?" Mom asked. "You mean you didn't tell them yet? Girl, when were you plannin' on askin' them? The party is almost here, and we need to know how much food to make. Lord knows, that Coop can eat," her mother said.

"I'll text him right now," Tarah said, relieved for an excuse to retreat to her bedroom, where her phone was charging.

"Here's another one that might work," Rochelle announced before Tarah could leave. She held up the book again so everyone could see it. "I think it's the best one. You're next to Aunt Deborah, Tarah, and you don't look that upset. See?"

Tarah leaned over to stare at the picture. A crowd of relatives stood in front of a stretch of trees. Aunts and uncles, some of them now deceased, smiled back at the camera. In front of them was a bunch of kids, including Rochelle, whose large toothy smile was visible from halfway across the room. Tarah spotted herself in the middle of the picture, standing right in front of Aunt Deborah. The old woman's hand rested gently on Tarah's shoulder as if she was trying to support her.

"Look how little you were," Kayla

said, gazing at the shot. "You're my size, Aunt Tarah."

It was true. Tarah noticed that the top of her head barely reached Aunt Deborah's chest. For a moment, she was struck to see how small she once was, not much bigger than the kids she watched at the daycare center where she worked over the summer. For a split second, Tarah imagined Kayla standing in the picture where she was, enduring the same pain. The thought made her cringe.

"And look how skinny we all were, too," Rochelle cackled, breaking her thoughts. "Would be nice to be that skinny again."

"Well, not *that* skinny," Mom huffed. "Y'all are fine the way you are."

Tarah rolled her eyes. She didn't want to talk about her weight, especially not now. No matter what Mom said, she knew she was heavy. Her hips and backside were what some called "thick," and men occasionally hollered about the "junk in her trunk" when she walked home from the bus stop. Most of the time, she was able to ignore the comments, the way she ignored the stink in the air after the bus passed by. And when the insults got to her, she had learned from Mom to mask the hurt behind a joke or a quick insult of her own.

"Never let them know they got to you or they'll just keep coming," Mom once said when Tarah was in second grade and a boy made her cry by calling her "jelly belly" at recess. *"And if you need to, go on and give 'em a taste of their own medicine. Most of them will leave you alone once you do that."*

Tarah had followed Mom's advice for years, and for the most part it had worked, allowing her to hide behind her jokes, her smile, and her loud cackling laughter. As she got older, she discovered she could hold her own in almost any crowd. At Bluford, this skill earned her respect and friends in different cliques, though there were still some who dismissed her or looked down on her. Tarah had learned to ignore them, too, and for a time she almost forgot the deep wounds from her childhood. But all that ended—shattered by the picture sitting in her cousin's lap: a photo of a skinny little girl about to cry.

"At least you don't look angry or mean in this one," Rochelle added.

"No," Kayla said, inspecting the picture as if it were a puzzle she was trying to solve. "You look scared and a little sad. How come, Aunt Tarah?"

Tarah wished she could rip the book away from them and burn it. She had wanted to do it years ago, to turn the photos to ash and erase any proof that the time had ever happened. It was what Mom did after Dad left to go back east when Tarah was a toddler. She had pulled out every picture of him and acted as if he never existed. Tarah wanted to do that, but she knew the pictures in this album were precious to her mother, especially the ones with the older relatives. Aunt Deborah was the oldest one left.

"I don't remember, Kayla," Tarah lied. "That was a long time ago."

"I don't know either," Mom said, "but that's certainly not how you usually were—or are. You may have been many things over the years, child, but scared is not one of them."

"It's true! That's why Coop always jokes that he's scared of her," Rochelle teased.

"If he knew what's good for him, he *would* be scared of her. My girl don't suffer no fools," Mom said with a laugh, giving Tarah a proud smile. "Me neither."

"Can you all please talk about something else?" Tarah said, doing her best to smile along with them. But inside, she felt exposed and vulnerable, like the child in the picture. She knew why she was so upset so many years ago, though no one else did.

Not her mother.

Not any of her many cousins.

Not her best friend at Bluford High School, Darcy Wills.

Not even Cooper Hodden.

"*I was scared that day, Momma,*" Tarah wanted to say, though she kept her mouth locked shut.

There was no way she would admit what happened the night before Aunt Linda's wedding, years ago, when many of her relatives were staying at her house. That night her uncle Rudy, a teenager at the time, had sat next to her on the sofa while the adults were in the other room cackling and laughing. She still recalled the odd way he had watched her and how he volunteered to babysit her and the younger cousins while the rest of the relatives went out celebrating. She could still remember the creak of his steps as he crept into her bedroom later that night after she had changed into her pajamas.

Rudy had taken the photo. Tarah could still see him in his baggy army-green shorts and black T-shirt standing behind the camera and eyeing her menacingly. Kayla was right to see fear in the picture, Tarah thought. She *had* been terrified.

"*I was afraid he'd hurt me again, Momma,*" she wanted to say, though she had decided long ago never to tell her or anyone else the truth. Ever.

It was a decision she revisited, a poison she had swallowed back down over the years whenever someone pulled out the old photographs and made her look at them.

"Oh my God, remember this guy?" Rochelle blurted. She had flipped the page and was looking at another photo. "What was his name? Uncle Rufus, right? I remember him. He was too young to be our uncle. He looks so handsome."

Tarah's stomach twisted. Her hands began to tremble, the way they did if she went all day without eating. She could feel Kayla staring at her, and she wondered if the little girl could tell she was upset.

"That's your Uncle Rudy, Rochelle,"

Mom said. "He was only about Tarah's age there."

"Whatever happened to him? We ain't seen him in, like, forever," Rochelle asked.

"That's 'cause he went down south to school and stayed in Atlanta since," Mom explained. "He's coming for Aunt Deborah's birthday, though."

"Really?" Rochelle asked.

Tarah felt as if the air had suddenly been sucked out of the house. She recoiled for an instant and bumped the edge of the end table, causing a glass of soda to spill in a fizzing mess on the floor in front of the sofa.

"Girl, watch it!" Rochelle yelled, squirming away from the spill before turning back to Tarah's mother. "Are you serious, Aunt Clarice? He's coming, too?"

"Of course he is! He's family," Mom exclaimed, eyeing Tarah curiously. "I invited him to stay here again, just like old times."

The room seemed to spin. Tarah's heart pounded in her chest and temples as she rushed to get a towel for the floor.

"You see, Kayla. It's just like I told you. You're going to meet all these new people in your family. Ain't that exciting?"

13

The little girl smiled and nodded.

Tarah wiped up the soda, barely hearing the small talk between her mother and her cousin until she heard Mom's voice directed at her.

"You okay, Tarah? You're awfully quiet today."

"I'm fine," she said, standing up from the floor, careful to avoid her mother's gaze. "I'ma call Coop and see if he's coming to the party. I'll be right back."

Tarah retreated to her room and closed the door, careful to keep her hands close to her body so no one could see them shaking.

Chapter 2

Where u at?

Tarah texted Cooper from her front stoop later that evening. She and Cooper had planned days ago to meet Darcy on Saturday night. They were all supposed to get pizza and then head to the movies. Tarah had been looking forward to going out all week, though she didn't really want to see *Zombie Storm*, the movie Cooper kept talking about.

But everything changed after Rochelle's visit. Even though Tarah escaped the house with Kayla for a while, she had been unable to shake the memories the photos had triggered. At one point, Kayla even asked her about it.

"What's wrong, Aunt Tarah?" the little girl had said, taking a break from playing with Kelena Mason, a little girl from down the street who often visited the park on weekends with her mom, Liselle. "Don't you want to sit on the swing with me?"

Tarah had been zoning out on a bench, leaving Kayla alone on the sliding board for a few minutes.

"Yeah, Kayla. You know I always want to play with you," she said, pretending it was a normal Saturday morning in early August. But whenever she closed her eyes, Tarah kept seeing Rudy's face. And then the thoughts would blast through her head like the music from the low-riders that sometimes circled the park.

He's coming back.

He's coming here.

I'm gonna have to face him.

The thoughts tormented her all day, making her edgy and nervous even as she sat on the stoop waiting for Cooper to arrive. Suddenly her phone began vibrating. Tarah jumped as Cooper's text message lit up the tiny screen.

Almost there

A minute later, his beat-up pickup truck pulled to a squeaky stop in front of her house.

16

"What's happenin', T?" Cooper asked as he emerged from the truck wearing a crisp white T-shirt and sagging indigo jean shorts that hung low so that they were nearly as long as pants. "Sorry I'm late, but you know how Larry Nye is. That dude is the first to complain if you're thirty seconds late. But if you stay a half hour extra cleanin' up that garage at the end of the night, he don't say a thing. Not even a thank you."

Tarah noticed that Cooper's shoulders seemed wider and the V-shape of his back broader than just a week or so ago. The weightlifting he had been doing for the upcoming football season was already making him look bigger. Just seeing him made her feel a little better.

"I told you you're the best thing to happen to that garage. Old Mr. Nye's gonna realize that once you cut your hours this fall for football. But that's okay. Serves him right," Tarah grumbled, trying to forget about what happened earlier. "C'mon, let's go. I been stuck here all day, and my mom and cousin have been drivin' me crazy."

Cooper leaned in for a kiss, and Tarah kissed him back quickly, though she found herself holding onto him for a second, pressing her face into his chest before letting him go.

"You okay? What's wrong, girl?"

For an instant, she imagined telling him what was upsetting her.

"There's something I never told you, Coop. Something that happened to me a long time ago . . ." But the words snagged in her throat.

"Nothing," she said instead. "Just my cousin and my mom. They all hyped about this party. But I ain't feelin' it. I mean why we gotta go gathering the whole family? There's only, like, three people I really want to see at this thing anyway."

"*Party?* You sure you feelin' all right? You're the last person I know to be hatin' on a party."

"This ain't a little friends thing, Coop. My family's havin' one of their big reunions for my great-aunt's birthday in a couple weeks. It's gonna be off the chain. Like almost a hundred people or something. Oh, that reminds me. You're comin', right? You can even bring Dez, too. There will be tons of food," Tarah added. Cooper's younger brother, Desmond, was going out with Darcy's little sister, Jamee, so Tarah figured she would invite them both.

"Yeah, I guess so, but I'm probably gonna be late."

"*Late?* Why?"

"Tarah, this is the first time you even told me about this thing. I got double practices for football the second half of August. I can't skip it unless I'm in the hospital or something. You know how Coach Meade is. Ain't no big thing. I'll just come over as soon as I'm done," Cooper explained. "Just save some food for me, all right? Speakin' of food, I'm starvin'! Can we go to Niko's? I'ma start eatin' my hand if I don't get some food quick."

"Is that all you can think about? Food?" Tarah snapped. She knew Cooper was right. Normally it wouldn't be a big deal if he were late for something. It actually happened all the time, and Tarah often teased him for it. But this was different. It meant she would be at the reunion without him, at least for a time.

"What? Girl, I'm serious. I ain't had nothin' to eat since breakfast."

"Whatever," she said, crossing her arms. She knew it wasn't his fault that she was upset. She wished she could just skip the party and never have to

19

think about it again.

"Seriously, can we talk about this later? If I don't eat soon, I'ma go zombie on you." Cooper then moaned and reached his arms out, zombie-style, dragging his leg behind him as they made their way toward his pickup. At the curb, he turned suddenly and grabbed her shoulder as if he was going to take a bite.

"Coop, would you quit playin'!" she snapped, shrugging him aside and getting into the truck.

"C'mon, Tarah!" Cooper teased, as he sat next to her in the driver's seat. "I'm just tryin' to get you in the mood. Remember? *Zombie Storm* tonight! You know you gonna get scared and cover your eyes. Just like you did at *Terror in the Streets.*"

He started the noisy truck and drove off.

"I wasn't scared. That movie was just dumb. Too dumb to watch, so I had to close my eyes," Tarah cut back. "Besides, you know I don't like scary movies. I don't even want to see no zombie film. I bet Darcy don't neither."

"Are you serious? After all them cheesy flicks you made me see? You remember the one about the friends who share their magic jeans?"

"That was good!" Tarah insisted, relieved to be talking about something besides the reunion. "Admit it. The part about the girl reuniting with her daddy had you all choked up. Don't even front. I remember you wipin' your eyes."

"That's because I was tryin' not to sleep! I had to do this just to keep my eyes open." Cooper then put his hand near his eye and pretended to prop his eyelid up. As he did, he looked at her for a second with a silly expression on his face. Though she didn't want to, she could feel herself beginning to smile. Before it happened, she slapped him playfully on the arm.

"You're crazy," she said, shaking her head.

"That's why you like me, right?" he asked, quickly grabbing her hand and holding it.

"Who said I liked you?" Tarah replied, gently squeezing his hand back. She smiled freely for the first time all day.

"Oh, it's gonna be like that now?"

"Isn't it always?"

"You're right. It is," he agreed, grinning back at her.

A crowd had already gathered in the multiplex lobby when they arrived. Cast in deep red and blue lights from the theater's overhead signs, people looked strange and zombie-like as they crammed in the ticket line. It seemed to Tarah as if half the city had decided to join them at the movies.

"This is gonna be *good*," Cooper said, rubbing his hands together in excitement.

"It better be," Tarah teased as they paid for their tickets.

"I wish Hakeem were here," Darcy added wistfully.

Uh oh. Here we go again, Tarah thought.

For days, Darcy had been unable to talk about anything except her ex-boyfriend, Hakeem Randall. The two broke up at the end of the school year when Hakeem moved with his family to Detroit to deal with his father's illness. Darcy had been devastated, but she had just learned that Hakeem was returning for his junior year at Bluford. Ever since then, she had been unable to talk about anything else.

"Hakeem'll be back next month. It's gonna be like old times again. I promise," Tarah said, trying her best to sound upbeat. She hoped her words would stop Darcy from rehashing how anxious she felt about him coming back. But she could see from the look on Darcy's face that she was wrong.

"I can't wait to see him. But I'm scared, Tarah," Darcy said. "What if we don't get back together? What if we're, like, all weird now. You know?"

It was the third time this week that they'd had this same conversation. Tarah felt bad for her, and she had tried her best to soothe Darcy's worries, including talking to her for an hour the other night. But now, after the day Tarah had, she wasn't in the mood to do it again.

"I'm not gonna lie, Darce. It's probably gonna be weird for a while, but you two will be all right. You'll see," Tarah insisted, hoping Darcy couldn't hear the weariness in her voice.

"But how do you know? I mean you know what I've been through this summer. What about him? Every time I ask him, he either changes the subject or acts all distant." Darcy again began

23

recounting her last discussion with him.

Tarah took a deep breath. If it were anyone else, she would have walked away, but this was Darcy, one of her closest friends at Bluford over the past year. Tarah couldn't just push her away, especially after the tough summer she had.

Besides losing her boyfriend and her grandmother, Darcy ran into trouble with Brian Mason, a nineteen-year-old who she had secretly hooked up with at the start of the summer. Tarah finally found out about it last month when Darcy revealed how the relationship ended.

"We started kissing," she had explained, fidgeting nervously with her cell phone as she talked. *"But then he started touching me. At first it was okay, but then it was too much. I told him no, but he wouldn't stop. Then he pinned me down . . . He was just so strong. If my dad hadn't shown up, I don't know what would have happened . . ."*

Tarah knew how Darcy felt. She didn't tell Darcy how upset the story made her or how it stirred her own painful memories. Instead, she helped Darcy find a counselor at the women's clinic near where she worked. Tarah had watched the steady stream of girls going there for help since the summer began. Occasionally, she imagined going in herself but always shrugged off the idea.

". . . I mean, I keep asking Hakeem to talk, but it's like he doesn't want to," Darcy continued, barely pausing to breathe. "Maybe it's just me, but sometimes I think he's hiding something . . ."

Tarah rubbed her forehead and suppressed a yawn. She tried to show Darcy the same interest she had given her the first time they had talked about Hakeem's return, but it was tough. Cooper rolled his eyes while Darcy's back was turned. After listening for a minute, he shrugged and escaped to the concession stand. Tarah ignored him. She knew he couldn't understand why Tarah felt so protective of Darcy, especially since the assault. Tarah knew Darcy wasn't aware of the bond they shared either, their secret pain, but it didn't matter. She could feel it even now, despite Darcy's endless talking.

"The other night he actually talked more about his cousin than anything else," Darcy complained, listing still more details Tarah had already heard.

Occasionally, Tarah nodded along and added a word or two, but mostly she just listened. It was what she had been doing with her friends and relatives for years. It seemed as if everyone would come to her to talk about their problems, as if she had none of her own.

"It's 'cause you got an old soul, Tarah. Just like Aunt Deborah," Mom said when she overheard her talking to Darcy one night.

Tarah didn't know about souls, but she did try her best to help her people. It made her feel good inside and blocked the dark memories that stalked her mind from time to time. Yet, as she listened to Darcy again, Tarah noticed that her friend didn't once stop to ask her how she was doing.

"Why would I care what his cousin is doing?" Darcy asked as if what Hakeem did was outrageous.

"I don't know—"

"Thank you! That's exactly what I mean," Darcy huffed. "We were supposed to go to the prom this year. Is that even gonna happen now? I can't imagine going with anyone else, but still . . ."

Tarah sucked her teeth. It was as if Darcy couldn't see anything except herself. And in a way, it felt the same way with Cooper tonight. Everything was about *his* movie. *His* hungry stomach. *His* plan.

Cooper returned with an enormous container of popcorn and led them toward the theater. Tarah could see he was purposely avoiding the conversation.

"I mean, this is our junior year already. Can you believe it? Seems like we just started yesterday . . ." Darcy went on and on.

Tarah half-listened as they entered the crowded theater. She spotted a few people from school, including Steve Morris, the annoying running back for Bluford's football team who acted as if he was the best athlete in the school. Maybe it was true, but that didn't give him the right to look down on everyone else the way he did. Tarah had seen it many times before. She knew Steve got on Cooper's nerves too, though now he hid it well.

"You ready for practice Monday?" Cooper called out to him.

"You know it!" Steve barked. "You better be faster this year if you're gonna block for me, Coop!"

Not far from Steve, Tarah recognized Shanetta Greene, a gossipy eleventh grader from Bluford's dance team. She wore jeans that flaunted her curvy backside, and for an instant Tarah noticed Cooper looking at her. Two other girls Tarah knew, Renita Jackson and Kym Reynolds, sat next to Shanetta texting on their phones and watching everyone who passed by.

Shanetta smirked as Tarah sat down. The two had known each other since grade school, though they weren't friends. Tarah hadn't trusted the girl ever since Shanetta boasted about stealing clothes from the mall when they were in fifth grade. Later she got a reputation for doing the same thing with boyfriends. In middle school, Tarah had heard rumors that Shanetta liked Cooper. It was a while ago, but Tarah hadn't forgotten about it.

"Look who it is," Tarah mumbled as they sat down.

"I saw her," Darcy answered back, stopping her endless talking about Hakeem for a minute. "Glad we're not sitting in their row."

"Me too. Zombies aren't the only things creepin' in this theater," Tarah mumbled as the previews started.

The lights dimmed and the murmuring crowd grew silent as *Zombie Storm* began. Tarah was glad to get a break from Darcy, though she wasn't looking forward to two hours of blood-and-gore on the big screen.

The movie started with a young girl alone in a dark bedroom. The girl heard rustling behind her closed door and sat up in her bed. Outside, the wind howled menacingly, and a distant rumble of thunder crackled far off. The little girl's eyes glinted in the darkness as something heavy moved in the hallway. The sound began to get louder and closer to her room.

The girl was scared, her eyes opened wide with terror.

Where were her parents? Tarah wondered, her heartbeat growing faster. Why did they leave her alone? Why wasn't anyone helping her?

Heavy steps thudded outside of the bedroom door. A large shadow appeared in the gap beneath the door.

Someone was standing in the hallway on the other side.

It was a view Tarah recognized. Maybe on another night she wouldn't have noticed. Maybe on another day, it wouldn't have bothered her. But as the scared little girl cowered in her bed, Tarah remembered the pictures from this morning. The memories suddenly gushed through her mind like blood from a wound.

The thud of footsteps in the hall. The shadows under her bedroom door. The greasy click of the doorknob turning.

Uncle Rudy creeping in.

Tarah could recall it all.

"Ahhhhh!" An earsplitting scream erupted behind them, from the back of the dark theater.

Tarah gasped and jumped, bumping into Cooper. He spilled some of his popcorn and cracked up laughing. So did several other people in the theater, including Shanetta, who pointed and whispered something to her friends.

In the back row, a group of guys cackled loudly and slapped hands.

"Relax. They just playin'. See, I knew you'd be scared," Cooper whispered.

Tarah glared back at them and then glanced up at the screen as the little girl's door was ripped from its hinges and a zombie entered her bedroom.

Tarah closed her eyes and sank into

her seat. She knew that the little girl's screams and the guys' joke were not real.

But the memories, the pounding of her heart, the sweat on her brow, and the tears in her eyes were.

What's happening to me? she thought to herself.

What's happening?

Chapter 3

"JJ, put that shovel down!" Tarah yelled.

It was late afternoon at Little Learning Spot, and Tarah and her supervisor, Ms. Stephanie, were in charge of the three-year-olds until parents arrived to pick them up. JJ, a light-skinned boy with a buzz cut, looked back at Tarah with a devilish glint in his eye. He held a red plastic shovel over his shoulder like a baseball bat, positioning himself near little Alexis as if he was going to swing it at the small girl's backside.

"You heard me, JJ," Tarah warned, quickly moving closer to him. "If you don't put it down, I'ma put you in time out until your daddy gets here." Her voice filled the small playground.

The little boy paused for a second,

dropped the shovel and ran off to a nearby swing set. Alexis smiled at Tarah as if to say thank you.

"How you doin', babygirl?" Tarah asked, giving Alexis a gentle hug. The little girl hugged her back, and for a second, Tarah almost felt like a normal person. But still, the thoughts of the reunion crept in her mind like a stalker.

A couple of days had passed since the episode at the movie theater. Tarah had spoken to Cooper a few times, but they never mentioned what happened. She knew that he and Darcy figured she had been startled by the screaming kids in the back of the theater. Tarah allowed them to think that and tried to forget about the entire night, but she couldn't shake that Aunt Deborah's party was now less than two weeks away. The idea haunted her on the playground as she watched her class of preschoolers.

"JJ is so quick!" exclaimed Ms. Stephanie. She was the newest teacher at Little Learning Spot and a few years older than Tarah's cousin Rochelle. She had a young son who also was a student in the toddler room at the school. "I mean he was standing with me one second, and the next thing I see is you stopping him from smacking Alexis. I hope my little man doesn't get that quick."

"Oh, he will," Tarah assured her. "Give him some time, that's all."

"I guess I better get faster, too," Ms. Stephanie said. "Good thing you saw him."

"Yeah, well, I got lotsa cousins, so I'm kinda used to how fast they are."

"Seriously, Tarah, I think you're great with the kids. They all love you. Even JJ! You ever think of being a teacher one day?"

"Me?" Tarah asked as Alexis ran off to play.

"Yeah, you! Why not? You're a natural with the kids. It's like you really care about them, and they know it. Look at Alexis," Stephanie said, nodding to where the little girl was playing. "She's one of the shyest girls in here, but she totally opens up to you. Around me, she's, like, '*Who is this strange lady talking to me?*' That's something you can't teach. It's just part of who you are. Trust me, I know. I did student teaching for two years and observed a lot of teachers."

Tarah blushed and smiled at Ms. Stephanie's compliment. She had never really thought about what might happen beyond high school. And the idea of being a teacher seemed crazy.

Darcy was the one who got A's in school and always talked about college. Tarah dismissed such plans because it all seemed so far away. Whenever she thought about "the future," she felt nervous and overwhelmed. Besides, she had never been more than an average student. Yet, as she thought about it, she knew that some of what Ms. Stephanie said was right. When it came to working with the kids, she was good. And she liked it, too—it was a chance to protect them and help them grow.

"Thanks," she replied, imagining for a second that she was at the head of a classroom with kids calling her *Ms. Carson*. "I never thought about it, but you never know."

"Well, start thinking. I'd even hire you to babysit my little Drew if you ever wanted to do it."

"Of course—I would love to!" Tarah replied, happy that the teacher trusted her with her own son. "Just let me know when."

Suddenly Tarah noticed a blur through the corner of her eye. She turned to see JJ dash through the playground.

"Boom!" he yelled, pretending to be Iron Man, his favorite cartoon character. He lunged playfully at other kids as if he were attacking them with metal fists and feet. He then eyed Alexis.

"Here he comes again," said Ms. Stephanie, watching him. Tarah moved protectively toward Alexis. The little girl looked nervous.

"Don't worry, baby. I gotcha," Tarah assured her.

"Just in time," said Ms. Stephanie, pointing to the street. "Look who's here." On the edge of the playground, Tarah spotted the silver Mazda that belonged to JJ's father. As they watched, he stepped out of the car wearing sunglasses and a backwards cap. Tarah could see that he was only a few years older than she was.

"Daddy!" JJ cheered as soon as he spotted him. The little boy darted across the playground to the edge of the fence to wait for his father. JJ's dad entered and hoisted the boy up over his shoulder, and pretending to punch him playfully, as if he were Iron Man, too.

"Like father, like son," Ms. Stephanie said as the two went to sign out at the front desk. "Boys will be boys."

Tarah sucked her teeth. "I guess.

But boys being boys don't mean they get to hit someone," Tarah mumbled so that only Stephanie could hear her.

"Looks like someone better let JJ's father know that," replied Ms. Stephanie.

"Good luck with that," Tarah grumbled, watching Alexis. She was annoyed at how easy it is for kids to be hurt, even at a safe place like school.

Again, the memories kicked and stirred inside her. She could almost hear the clock ticking as the reunion loomed closer. Soon Uncle Rudy would make his way across the country toward her.

"I know who can do it one day," Ms. Stephanie said.

"Who?" Tarah asked, angered that she was thinking about Aunt Deborah's party again.

"You," Ms. Stephanie said with a glimmer in her eye. "When you become a teacher."

Check it. Whos da man?

The text arrived as Tarah sat watching TV later that night. The sender was Cooper. It was followed seconds later by a picture.

Tarah clicked to enlarge the image. It

was Cooper standing outside of Bluford High School. He had started football practice this week, and the picture looked as if it was taken after practice was over.

Cooper was wearing a white tank top and glistening with sweat. He was flexing like a weightlifter and making a fake grimace as if he were straining himself. But what stood out was his body. His dark shoulders and arms rippled with muscle. He looked chiseled, like a statue from an old history book. She had to admit he was beautiful, and she told him that in a text right back.

Lookn gooood!!!

His reply was instant.

Thx—no zombies gonna get u while Im here ;)

She glanced at the picture again. Steve Morris and several other football players were flexing in the shot, too. Behind them, two girls were pointing at Cooper. *Who were they?* Tarah wondered. Suddenly, she found herself inspecting the picture closely.

She recognized two girls from the dance team right away. They stood watching as Cooper showed off for the camera. One face Tarah didn't see was Shanetta's. Tarah remembered how she supposedly had a crush on Cooper back in eighth grade. Had she been there when the shot was taken?

Tarah remembered Shanetta's fake smile from the night at the movie theater and cringed. The girl reminded her of a wolf.

Was she looking at Coop's body?

Who had taken the picture?

The questions bubbled in Tarah's head as she stared at the tiny screen on her phone. She needed to know. Now.

Quickly her thumbs became a blur as she began to text him the question. Halfway through, she scrapped the message and dialed Cooper's cell. It rang twice and then he picked up.

"Who were you with today?" she asked as soon as she heard his voice.

"Huh?"

"Today when you was messin' around for everybody at school. Who was there?"

"Girl, we ain't talked all day and this is how you say hello?"

Tarah knew he was right, but she couldn't help it. Besides, he knew she didn't trust Shanetta. They had talked about it once before.

"Tell me it wasn't Shanetta Greene."

"C'mon, Tarah. Why you so upset?"

"Was it her?"

Cooper paused. She knew his answer before he said the words.

"Yeah, but it ain't no big thing, okay?"

"So you wouldn't be upset if some boy that used to like me started taking pictures of me when you weren't there?"

Tarah winced inside as she listened to Cooper's stammering answer. She knew, even as he spoke, that there was no use comparing herself to him. There was no one vying for her attention or wanting to take pictures of her. Given her size, people would laugh if someone even suggested it, she figured. One of those laughing would be Shanetta Greene, with her round behind, dancer's legs, and flawless cinnamon skin. Tarah knew that Cooper thought Shanetta looked good. How couldn't he?

"All I'm saying is that this ain't some-thin' to get upset about, okay?" Cooper insisted. "There were lots of people outside after practice and some of the girls from the dance team started coming in 'cause they practice right after us," he explained. His voice was a little forced, the way it got when he felt guilty about something.

"Mmm hmm."

"So Steve Morris was sayin' all this stuff about how ripped I looked, so, you know, I started flexin' and—"

"And then Shanetta came over and took your picture."

"It wasn't just like that. Why you go twisting things?"

"What'd she say? Did she say you look good? Go on. You can tell me."

"See, there you go again. C'mon, Tarah! I ain't with her. I'm with you. I sent you the picture, didn't I? Would I do that if I was tryin' to hide somethin'?"

Tarah took a deep breath. She knew what Cooper said made sense. And in the year they had been together, he had never given her any reason to doubt him before. Yet there was a gnawing feeling inside her, one she knew was connected somehow to the reunion.

"I don't care what you say, Cooper. There ain't no way I'm gonna like getting pictures of my boyfriend's body taken by some girl that wants to get with him, okay? Can you understand what I'm saying?"

41

"But can't you hear me? There's nothin' to worry about, okay?"

She tried to focus on his words, but she couldn't help thinking about Shanetta. What if he secretly liked her? What if he would rather be with the curvy girl than her, someone who weighed almost as much as he did? Someone who carried a secret so ugly that she was too ashamed to tell him?

Most days, Tarah was able to hide these thoughts far from Cooper and even herself. But now, with the reunion closing in, they were stronger than ever. They made her feel vulnerable and jealous and insecure. They made her hurt, too.

"I'm sorry, Coop," she wanted to say. *"It's not you. It's me. Something happened to me a long time ago."* But fear and shame, like two invisible hands, gripped her throat and held the words inside.

She kept imagining what would happen if she told him. Would he leave her the way her father had abandoned their family so long ago? Would he think she was ugly or disgusting? Would he not even be able to look at her anymore? Would he see her as she sometimes saw herself? The ugly words slashed at her like blades.

Fat. Ugly. Ashamed. Abused.

Tarah's skull ached and her stomach turned.

"Look, Tarah, I'm sorry," Cooper said, breaking the awkward silence that had wedged itself between them. "You're right. That was kinda stupid now that I think about it."

"Yeah, it was stupid," she said, telling him she had to go and then abruptly hanging up.

For hours, Tarah lay in her bed, rocking herself back and forth as she did that night years ago, hot tears slipping silently down her face.

Chapter 4

Tarah sat in the hazy morning sun on the Bluford bleachers and watched Cooper sprint across the goal line at football practice, his arms raised in triumph.

"That's right, Coop!" she screamed, but he didn't seem to hear her. Instead, he bumped fists with Steve Morris and headed right to a bench on the sidelines.

Shanetta Greene was sitting there alone, wearing a cropped tank top that revealed a section of her stomach. It was taut, smooth, and muscular, and Tarah could see Cooper pull off his helmet and focus right on her.

"Whatchu doin', Coop?" Tarah yelled, but he ignored her. Instead, he sat next to Shanetta, and she gave him that toothy, wolfish smile and leaned into him, her arm wrapping around his back.

"Coop!" Tarah yelled, rising from the bleacher in time to see him turn his head toward Shanetta.

"Coop! Why are you ignoring me? Why can't you hear me?"

Shanetta craned her head upward, and suddenly the two of them kissed, their lips gently pressing together.

Tarah felt the ground sink beneath her feet. It was as if an invisible hand had grabbed her heart and was crushing it.

It was true, she realized. Shanetta had taken him away. He was gone.

No!

Waves of rage and sorrow and defeat crashed through her, leaving her broken and alone. Overhead, the sun, swollen and red, glared down at her like an angry eyeball.

Suddenly she heard footsteps.

How long had she been there? The football field was completely empty. The school looked abandoned, and she realized that her voice was gone. She couldn't make a sound.

She felt a heavy thud on the bleacher and looked up to see a man approaching.

It was Uncle Rudy.

No!

Tarah bolted upright in her bed and

45

gasped for breath, her body slick with sweat, her heart pounding like a drum as the dream evaporated.

"Girl, what's wrong with you?" Tarah whispered to herself in the darkness.

On the bed next to her, she saw her cell phone flash with a text from Cooper that had arrived several hours ago. She realized she had slept right through it.

Out w Steve Morris n some guys from the team. Talk ltr.

Tarah read the text several times and had an uneasy feeling. Cooper never hung out with Steve Morris, though he was in the background of the picture Shanetta took.

Had Shanetta gone out with them, too?

Tarah felt a sinking feeling in the pit of her stomach.

Don't do this to me, Cooper, she thought. *Please don't do this to me.*

The late-day August sun scorched the sidewalk as Tarah sat down on the small bench outside Scoops, the ice cream shop where Darcy worked. It was just past 6:00 p.m. on Tuesday, the time she and Darcy always met.

"Girl, I need to talk to you," Tarah said as soon as her friend stepped out, still wearing her uniform from work. "It's about Coop."

"Coop? What happened?" Darcy asked, handing Tarah a large mint chocolate chip milkshake. On Tuesdays, Darcy got them free, and the two would meet outside and enjoy them as they walked home. "It isn't Larry Nye again, is it?"

"Nah, it's worse," Tarah mumbled, sipping her shake. All day, she had been thinking about Cooper and the odd text he had sent. Shanetta had crossed a line, even if Cooper couldn't see it. It was as if she was testing to see how far she could go. "It's Shanetta Green. She's goin' after Coop," Tarah huffed.

"What?!" Darcy exclaimed. "Are you sure?"

Tarah explained about the cell phone picture and how Shanetta had complimented him. Then she mentioned how the girl used to like Cooper in eighth grade.

"Well, I can see why you'd be upset," Darcy said as they neared her house. "But I don't think you've got anything to worry about. This is Coop! I see the way

47

he looks at you. He's not interested in anyone else, Tarah. He probably didn't even notice what Shanetta was doing until after it was already done. You know how Coop is."

"Yeah, I know. That's kinda what he said too, but this is Shanetta. She used to steal from Mr. Kim's grocery store in fifth grade like it was nothin'. That girl takes what she wants. And right now, I know what she wants—Coop."

"You really think she's like that?" Darcy asked between sips of her strawberry shake.

"I know she is. That's why I didn't invite her to my birthday party last April. Remember? I wouldn't trust her as far as I could throw her."

"But she's not going to get anywhere with him, Tarah. You don't have to worry. If she hasn't figured that out yet, she will soon. Shanetta's just wasting her time."

"So are you sayin' I should just do nothin' about it?" Tarah grumbled, unable to hide her frustration.

"Well, did you talk to Coop about it? I mean maybe he just needs to make it clear to her that he's not interested. If he does that, this whole thing is solved, right?"

"You know Coop. He's not gonna do that," Tarah fumed. "I'm thinkin' I should have a word with her myself, you know? Why should I wait for him, when I can take care of it?"

"You really think that's a good idea? That might make things worse," Darcy said. "I really think you should just talk to Coop. Tell him this is important to you. He'll listen to you and shut this whole thing down. You'll see."

Tarah wanted to believe the words were true, but she couldn't shake the image of Shanetta's smiling face from her mind, or the strange way Cooper had gone out with Steve Morris in the middle of the night. What if Darcy was wrong? What if Cooper was hiding things from her?

He ain't the only one who's hiding something, Tarah thought bitterly to herself. Again, her thoughts turned to the reunion. She hadn't mentioned it to Darcy yet.

The two girls stopped in front of Darcy's house. Tarah stared at the small sun-dried patch of grass and suddenly felt a knot in the pit of her stomach. She couldn't bring herself to admit the real reason she wanted Darcy at the party.

Instead, she took a quick sip of her milk-shake and tried her best to stay calm.

"So whatchu doin' next Saturday?" she asked.

"I don't know. Why?"

"My family's having this big reunion. Lots of people are coming, and we're gonna be in Municipal Park doin' the whole barbecue thing. Friends and family are invited and . . ." She paused, trying to hide how nervous and unsettling the conversation made her. "I mean, it's gonna be crazy, and I just really would like for you to be there, you know, just so I can escape from my family."

"Sure, I'll be there," Darcy agreed, and Tarah immediately felt relieved, but then her friend squinted as if she smelled something strange. "Wait, did you say *next* Saturday?"

"Yeah, why?"

"Sorry, girl. I just remembered we're supposed to go to my Aunt Charlotte's that afternoon for dinner. Believe me, I don't want to go, but—"

"Can't you just get out of it? Please? I mean, just say you got plans or some-thin'," Tarah urged. She hated the way her voice sounded as if she was begging Darcy to be there, but she couldn't help it. *I ain't never asked anything like this from you before, but I need you to be there,* she wanted to add.

"Girl, you know I want to. I can't stand going to my aunt's house. It always ends up with my sister shouting at her and my mom getting all upset and all this drama. But since my grandma died, my aunt keeps trying to see us. And I can tell it's really important to my mom. We even had a big talk about it the other night," Darcy explained. "How about Sunday instead?"

Tarah sighed and shook her head. "No, it's okay."

"Sorry, Tarah, but my mom scheduled this and you never told me—"

"Fine," she said coldly, turning away from her friend. "I gotta go." Tarah began walking down the block, gulping her milkshake as she moved.

"Tarah?"

Tarah ignored her and kept walking.

"Are you all right?" Darcy called out. "What's wrong?"

"Nothing," Tarah said, feeling a mix of anger and frustration at her friend. "I just gotta go. I'll talk to you later."

"Tarah?"

"I gotta go!" she yelled, hurrying away

51

from Darcy's house, feeling as if her two closest friends were abandoning her when she most needed them.

Minutes later, Tarah slouched in a seat on the bus as it rumbled back toward her house. Nearby, two older teenage boys cackled about the passengers on the bus and started talking about her.

"Man, look at that girl!" the one boy said just loud enough for her to hear. "She keep drinkin' them shakes, and she's gonna be supersized!"

"She already there, yo!"

Tarah wanted to dump the last of the milkshake on the two wiry boys with their pointy chins and baggy clothes. But her stop was next, and after everything, she felt like the little girl in her mom's photo book, alone and scared. The truth kept pressing on her like the heat outside.

Rudy was coming.

Cooper and Darcy wouldn't be there.

No one knew the truth. No one except Tarah and Rudy.

Tarah quickly rushed off the bus, unable to silence the pointed laughter that pierced her like bee stings as she made her way onto the hot street.

She decided to stop by Aunt Lucille's house rather than go straight home. She really needed to see Kayla. The little girl could cheer her up when things were bad.

"Where's my girl?" Tarah asked, knocking on her aunt's door.

"Here I am, Aunt Tarah," Kayla called out, unlocking the door. She was wearing pink shorts and a white tank top with balloons printed on it, and her hair was pulled back into pigtails tied in pink ribbons.

"How you doin', Kayla!" Tarah boomed as she walked in. Kayla gave Tarah a sticky hug and then rushed back to the couch to watch TV. Inside the familiar living room, a large floor fan stirred the soupy August air but offered little relief from the heat.

"Hey, Tarah," Rochelle said, sitting across from her folding laundry. "So you ready for the big day? A little more than a week till the circus comes to town," she joked, referring to the party. "I'm actually kinda excited."

"To be honest, I'm really not feelin' it right now," Tarah admitted.

"Why not? You normally all about gettin' together. Why you so down on this?"

You don't even want to know, Tarah almost said. "I just got a lot on my mind, that's all."

"Like what? Girl, you only sixteen years old and in high school. What could you possibly have on your mind that's so heavy?"

"Oh, just 'cause I'm younger means I don't got anything to worry about?"

"There you go again! For about a month I swear you been like a different person. All I'm sayin' is you got it easy, okay?" she said, gesturing toward Kayla, who was staring glaze-eyed at the TV screen. "Try being on duty 24-7. Then you'll understand how easy you got it now."

Tarah bit her tongue. She knew it was tough to take care of kids, but from what she could see, Rochelle seemed to get lots of help from other people, including Tarah and Aunt Lucille. But she wasn't going to argue with Rochelle about it in front of Kayla. "Whatever," she grumbled.

"What, you got problems with Cooper or something?"

Tarah took a deep breath and sucked her teeth.

"That's it, isn't it?" Rochelle suddenly

54

leaned forward in interest. Tarah realized that her face had given away the answer.

"It's part of it," she grumbled.

"For real? Oh, now *this* I gotta hear. Go on, girl. Tell me what's up."

Tarah reluctantly told Rochelle everything she had mentioned to Darcy.

"Oh, you need to tell that Shanetta to step off," Rochelle said, shaking her head adamantly as she spoke. "The sooner you do it, the better, too."

"You think so?" Tarah asked. She wasn't surprised that Rochelle's advice was so different than Darcy's. Rochelle always had stormy relationships, but Tarah thought it was because she had bad taste in guys. No one she ever brought home was anywhere near the man Cooper is, especially Kayla's father, Aaron, who hadn't visited his daughter in six months.

"Definitely. If you don't protect what's yours, she gonna come in and take it. Trust me. I know. That's what happened to me."

Rochelle then went into a long story about how, in high school, her boyfriend was drinking at some party and this other girl, who was supposed to be her friend, hooked up with him.

"She knew just what she was doing. I seen her watching him in school and then she waited until I wasn't around and *BOOM!* She moved in."

"Yeah, but isn't it just as much *his* fault? I mean if he was someone you could trust, then you wouldn'ta had to worry. And if he wasn't someone you could trust, you probably better off without him, right? I mean, it ain't all the girl's fault. The guy has to do something. I mean this is Coop," Tarah said, repeating what Darcy had said to her.

Rochelle shook her head. "Tarah, you got a lot to learn, okay? Maybe in the movies or something, guys are perfect like you described. But in reality, if a girl's tryin' to steal your man, you gotta do something about it. That's just the way it is."

Tarah rubbed her temples. She could feel another headache coming. She knew Rochelle believed what she said, but it didn't match what she knew about Cooper. He was the same guy who showed up early one morning to repair Mom's car after someone broke into it and ripped out the stereo. None of Rochelle's boyfriends were like that.

They probably the ones that robbed

the car, Tarah thought to herself.

"By the way, is Coop comin' Saturday?" Rochelle asked, breaking Tarah's thoughts.

"Yeah, but he's gonna be late. He's got double practices for football," Tarah answered, unable to hide how much the news bothered her.

Just then Tarah felt her phone start to buzz. It was a call from Darcy. For a second, Tarah was about to let it go to voicemail, but then she decided to take it.

"Yeah?" she answered, still angry that she wasn't coming to the reunion.

"Listen, Tarah, I just spoke to Jamee, and she was watching movies last night at Dez and Coop's."

"So?" What did Cooper's little brother have to do with anything? Tarah wondered.

"Well, she saw Coop rush out last night. Turns out, he was picking up Shanetta."

"What?!" Tarah felt as if her legs might buckle. She knew Rochelle was listening, trying to pick up every word, but Tarah couldn't hide her surprise.

"It might not mean anything. Jamee didn't know any details. She was just telling me what Dez told her. Maybe it's

57

nothing, but after everything we were talking about, I thought you should know," Darcy paused as if she knew the news would be hard for her to bear. "Look Tarah, about the barbecue next week, I'm really sorry I can't be there—"

"Let's talk about this later," Tarah said, cutting her off. "I'll call you back." She hung up the phone before Darcy could say another word. For a second, she sat motionless, staring at the phone in her trembling fingers.

"That was about Coop, wasn't it?" Rochelle asked.

Tarah nodded.

"I told you," she said. "Next time you'll listen to me."

Tarah couldn't speak. Her world had suddenly shifted, and everything she knew and trusted seemed to be coming apart. She looked at Rochelle's scowl and felt, for once, that her cousin had given her good advice.

It was time to fight.

Chapter 5

Tarah forced herself out of bed early the next morning and inspected her face in the bathroom mirror. Her eyes were bloodshot and puffy from barely sleeping the night before. A line of pimples dotted her scalp just beneath her hairline. Even her face seemed fuller than usual to her, as if the stress was piling up inside, inflating her like a balloon.

"Girl, you gotta lose this," she said to herself, pushing her cheeks in as if she could somehow squeeze out the weight in her face.

After a quick shower, she spent nearly an hour on her hair, combing it out over and over to get it straight and parted before using her mother's flat iron to style it. She fixed it carefully so it framed her face just right. When her hair was done, she covered each blemish with makeup so she looked her best. Then she put on her favorite outfit that made her full body look more curvy and less frumpy. She had to be at work by noon, but she had somewhere else to go first.

"If we gonna do this, we gonna do it right," she mumbled as she looked at the time on her cell phone. Football practice was already over for the day. The dance team would finish their practice soon. To meet Shanetta, she had to leave now.

Cooper had no idea of her plan. She had spoken to him the night before and waited for him to mention that he had been alone in his truck with Shanetta, but he never said a word about it.

"Why you so quiet tonight?" he had asked when they were on the phone.

"Tired, I guess," she lied, hiding how worried she was about what he did. The fact that he didn't say anything, she figured, meant it was serious. "How about you? How was Steve Morris?" she had asked, hoping Cooper would admit what happened or where he had gone the other night.

"Man, that dude is just as annoying as usual," Cooper grumbled but then seemed to stop himself. "You know he wants me to install some system in his car so he can roll up and down the street shaking everybody's windows. Do I got a sign on my shirt that says I work at Best Buy?!" Cooper had complained, his voice a little too forced and unnatural. Tarah could hear it as if it was an off-key singer at church, yet she remained quiet and let Cooper talk.

The whole time she hoped he would bring up Shanetta Green, but he didn't. When he finally hung up, Tarah still couldn't believe what Darcy had told her—that Cooper had snuck out in the middle of the night with that girl, that he had betrayed Tarah, that he had practically lied to her face about what he had done.

"Tarah, you got a lot to learn." Rochelle's words echoed in her mind.

Maybe Cooper was a dog, just like Rochelle's boyfriends. Maybe he had played Tarah many times before and she didn't know it. She started to feel sick, as if he had mugged her and stole her trust and her heart. She pictured Shanetta sitting next to Cooper in his pickup, with its scuffed dashboard and rattling windows. Had he held Shanetta's hand as they drove, making his silly jokes, and carrying on until she leaned in to kiss him? The image made Tarah furious, and she had to fight to keep her anger in check. She couldn't go down that path, not until she saw Shanetta first. That would answer all her questions at once. Tarah was sure of it.

Without texting or calling Cooper, she got on the usual number 39 bus and took the ten-minute ride to the stop across from SuperFoods, the grocery store down the street from Bluford High. It was just after 10:00 a.m. when she stepped off at the plexiglass bus stop covered in magic-marker graffiti. The bus thundered and groaned as it pulled away in a smelly cloud of diesel smoke. Tarah gazed at Bluford High looming in the distance.

In a month, she would be back at the school, ready to start her junior year, but it felt strange to be there in the summer. The fenced-in lot on the side of the school was nearly empty, and the usual traffic of kids walking around the school was gone. Even the basketball courts were silent and the gates that led to them were locked with heavy metal chains, making the whole place seem like an abandoned prison.

She approached the school alone and

stopped at the bottom of the steps that led to the main entrance. For a second, she paused and looked at the time on her phone. She knew Shanetta's practice had just ended.

Just then, the front door of the school opened slowly, and old Mr. Watkins, one of the school janitors, stepped out.

"Can I help you, ma'am?" he asked, squinting from the sunlight as he stood at the top of the steps that led to the front door. "You here for the teacher interview with Principal Spencer?"

Teacher interview? Despite everything, Tarah almost laughed.

"Nah, I'm meeting someone from the dance team. It's me, Mr. Watkins. Tarah Carson."

"Tarah?!" the old man said with a smile. "Is that you? Why, from here, you look just like a teacher! Ms. Spencer's been interviewing them all week. Maybe you should apply for the job," he joked.

"Maybe one day," she said with a weak smile.

"Well, them girls at practice should be out any minute. You wanna come in?"

"No, I'ma wait out here," Tarah said, thinking it was safer if she was away from where Principal Spencer might observe them.

Just then, girls' voices boomed from inside the school. Tarah's palms began to sweat, and instinctively she turned slightly and clenched her fists.

"Here they come now," Mr. Watkins said before disappearing back inside.

Tarah looked on as clusters of girls in shorts and T-shirts emerged from the school. Some of them were familiar to her, but others were complete strangers.

"Yo, whatchu doin' here, Tarah?" asked Latisha Daniels, a girl Tarah knew from church.

"I gotta talk to someone."

"Mmm hmm. It ain't Shanetta, is it?"

"Yeah. Why?"

"I ain't sayin' nothin'," she said, looking over her shoulder.

"But you just did," Tarah huffed as Latisha strolled away.

Just then, the big steel doors swung open, and three girls barged through the doorway, deep in conversation as they emerged from the school.

"So whatchu gonna do about it?" the first one asked.

"Nothin'," said Shanetta, walking between the other girls. "I don't want anything to do with him no more. I don't know what I was thinking seeing him to begin with. I shoulda listened to you. You were right, Monica," she confessed.

Shanetta wore spandex shorts and a loose white tank top. A black sports bra was visible under the low neckline of her shirt, and the sides of the tank top were open, showing a small portion of her muscular stomach.

"He's a dog. Ain't no one gonna believe what he says," said the third girl, whose hair was pulled back in a tight ponytail.

"What if you're wrong, Aisha? You know how everyone at Bluford is," Shanetta snapped. "I can't believe this is happening."

None of them seemed to notice Tarah standing at the bottom of the steps. Tarah felt self-conscious as the three shapely dancers neared her. What could she do if Cooper really wanted to be with Shanetta, Tarah wondered. Nothing, she figured bitterly. But she couldn't just sit there and wait for Cooper to leave her the way Rochelle's boyfriends had left.

"I can't believe it either," Tarah said then, belting the words from deep in her chest. She could feel her pulse throb in

65

her temples. Anger flared in her chest.

"Huh?" Aisha said.

"Who is *that?*" asked Monica.

Shanetta took a step back as if to brace herself. "Whatchu want, Tarah?"

"What do I want?" Tarah repeated, as if the question were silly. "What I *want* is for you to stay away from my boyfriend."

"What?" Shanetta's eyes grew wide as if she was surprised at the accusation.

"Don't act like you don't know what I'm talking about!" Tarah yelled. "You know you been tryin' to get with him since eighth grade. That's right, I remember."

"What's she talkin' about Shay?"

Shanetta ignored the question. "Tarah, I don't know who you been talking to, but you got your facts all wrong," she said, pausing to look back at the school, as if she was concerned someone was watching. "Besides, if I wanted to steal your boyfriend—which I don't—you couldn't stop me. Look at you."

The comment hit Tarah like a slap. Shanetta's friends smiled. Aisha struggled to hold back laughter.

Tarah knew that it wasn't smart confronting Shanetta this way, outnumbered and without anyone knowing where she was. But she didn't care. Anger drove her forward, urging her to go after Shanetta, to smack the toothy smile from her face. And yet Shanetta's comment held her still, just for a second longer.

"Girl, I seen them pictures you took. Don't try to lie to me, okay? I know who you are, Shanetta. I remember back in the day how you used to steal the things you wanted like they belonged to you. Maybe on 43rd Street that's okay. But that ain't right by me. Now maybe your new friends don't know you, but I do. Ain't no sense lying to me, 'cause I see through it all. So I'ma tell you this one time: Stay away from Coop. You hear me? You ain't got no business messin' with him."

Shanetta recoiled as if what Tarah said stung her. Her friends were suddenly silent, as if the words they just heard surprised them somehow.

"Whatchu know about me? Huh?" Shanetta demanded.

Tarah was unprepared for the question and for a second didn't know what to say.

"That's what I thought. You don't know nothin'," Shanetta fumed, putting her hand on her hip. "Like I said, I ain't interested in Cooper. If you asked him, he'd tell you that, too, but you too busy gettin' in my face to notice you got it all wrong."

"Then why were you out with him last night?"

The two girls looked at each other and then at Shanetta. She could see in their eyes that they knew the answer.

"Why should I tell you? You're the one that knows everything, right? Why don't you ask Coop? Did you even do that?"

"It ain't none of your business what Coop and I talk about," Tarah barked, unwilling to admit anything to them.

"It *is* my business if you're gettin' in my face. I'm sick of you and everyone else thinking the worst about me 'cause a where I live or what I did years ago. None of y'all know what I had to deal with at home all those years I was takin' stuff. Be glad you weren't like me, okay?" she said.

For an instant, Shanetta almost seemed hurt. It was a side of her that Tarah had never seen before. Somehow, the angry girl almost made her feel guilty.

"You ain't the only one who's had it rough," Tarah cut in, wondering what Shanetta had dealt with that made her so upset.

"I never said I was. But you . . . I actually thought you were better than that, Tarah, but I guess I was wrong. You judged me just like everybody else. It's 'cause I live on 43rd Street, right? Or maybe 'cause I dance? Is that it? You as bad as the dumb boys thinking they can get with me just 'cause a some rumor they heard. I ain't interested in Cooper, okay? And you need to stop actin' like you better than me. You ain't no better. Only bigger," she huffed, before turning and walking away.

Tarah cursed under her breath. Part of her still wanted to shove the smaller girl to the sidewalk in front of her friends. But another part of her felt ashamed. Until now, she had no idea Shanetta carried scars too, but after listening to her, she knew they were there.

And what about Cooper? Shanetta didn't deny she was out with him. What had he been doing with her that he didn't want to admit? Why hadn't Tarah just asked him instead of sneaking around to confront Shanetta? The more she thought about it, the more she wished she hadn't even come to Bluford at all that day.

"All finished with the principal, Ms.

Carson?" The scratchy voice broke her thoughts. It was old Mr. Watkins lumbering slowly down the steps. He smiled pleasantly as if he liked the joke he had with her. "I'm telling you. One day, maybe you'll be teaching here like that Mr. Mitchell."

"I don't know, Mr. Watkins," she replied with a weak smile as he made his way toward the staff parking lot. "I don't feel like a teacher. Not today," she added.

"You'll get there," he said as he passed her. "You're on your way right now. I can tell."

All afternoon, people at Little Learning Spot kept telling Tarah how nice she looked, but inside she didn't feel nice. Instead, she felt guilty and irritable and worried.

"Look at you!" said Ms. Stephanie as they took the kids out for the afternoon. "You look great!"

"Thanks," Tarah mumbled, doing her best to keep an eye on the kids at the playground.

"You know, I been thinking about what we talked about earlier in the week. If you're still willing to babysit Drew for me, that would be great," Ms.

Stephanie said after most of the kids had left for the day.

"Yeah, I'd love to do it," Tarah replied, trying her best to sound enthusiastic. "When you need me?"

"Well, my husband and I want to go out to dinner. Since Drew was born, we haven't gone out once in about a year and a half. If you could babysit this Saturday or next Saturday, that would be great. Whatever's better for you."

Tarah paused for a moment as the request sank in. Next Saturday was when Aunt Deborah's party was scheduled. If she worked that day babysitting, she wouldn't be able to attend the reunion. The thought made her heart swell. It was the first piece of good news she had in weeks.

A perfect excuse to skip the party. A way to avoid having to face Uncle Rudy again. A way to escape what had been stalking her mind for days. A way out.

"Next Saturday is good for me," Tarah said, feeling relief spread over her.

"Are you sure?" said Ms. Stephanie, her voice swelling with happiness. "'Cause if it's not good, we could do it another weekend. I know it's short notice."

"Nah, it works for me," Tarah said. "Next Saturday is perfect, actually."

"Great!" the teacher cheered, thanking Tarah and giving her a slip of paper. "Here's my address and phone number. I'm so glad you can do this!"

Me too, she thought to herself, clutching the piece of paper as if it were a lifeline. She finally had a way out. In a little more than a week, Rudy would come and go, and Tarah wouldn't have to see him.

Thank you, God, she thought to herself as more parents arrived to pick up their kids. *Thank you!*

"Who's that? I never saw him before," Ms. Stephanie said. Tarah followed her gaze to a familiar pickup truck parked on the street. Inside, she saw Cooper staring right at her, his eyes unusually serious.

"He's here for me," Tarah said, her stomach suddenly sinking. "That's my boyfriend."

Chapter 6

"I thought you had to work today," Tarah said, shutting the truck's heavy door with a loud thud. She inspected her face in the mirror and thought for a second she smelled a trace of perfume in the air. Did it belong to Shanetta?

Tarah couldn't believe that girl had sat in her seat just two nights ago. Why had Cooper hidden it from her? Was it that he liked Shanetta, even though she wasn't interested in him? Or had Shanetta lied to her? Tarah had to find out the truth, even if it was going to hurt.

"I did work today, but I left early so I could come here and see you," Cooper explained, steering the rattling pickup truck onto the steamy street. The late afternoon sun pounded down on them as they waited at a traffic light. "Besides, if

I had to listen to Larry Nye for one more minute today, I was gonna lose it."

"I know the feeling," said Tarah, trying to read Cooper's face. Was this it? Did he take off work early to have "the talk" with her? Would he admit his feelings for Shanetta and break up with her? Tarah still couldn't believe he would do such a thing. And yet, she could see he was tense, chewing on his lip as he drove.

Suddenly, bass thundered in the air and rattled the hood of Cooper's truck. It boomed from a gold Nissan that darted in front of them from a side street and raced up the block. Tarah felt the rhythmic pulse in her stomach. A child on the sidewalk put her hands to her ears as the sedan zoomed past.

"This ain't no club. It's a street!" Tarah complained as the sound slowly died off.

"That's what Steve wants me to put in his car," Cooper admitted. "He said he'd pay me fifty bucks to do it for him."

"If you ask me, that boy is loud enough by himself. He don't need no system makin' it worse."

"You don't know the half of it," Cooper said, eyeing her strangely before turning the truck onto a highway entrance ramp. "Seen him too much since football practice started," he said, hitting the gas. "Way too much."

The old pickup shuddered as it climbed the ramp and merged onto the highway. Tarah squinted at the bright sun and looked down on the steamy neighborhood. Car windshields glimmered in the streets below like sparks in some giant fire. It was as if the whole city was boiling before her. She could make out Bluford High School in the distance. It seemed tiny, dwarfed by the endless blocks of the city. It was a view that always surprised her. For so long, Bluford had seemed huge. The center of everything. A whole world in itself.

It wasn't until she started driving with Cooper that she began to see that her own neighborhood was just a small part of the city, that there were other sections nothing like her own. Sometimes she dreamed of just jumping in the truck with Cooper and leaving it all behind. The neighborhood. The school. The memories. They had even discussed it a few times, just driving forever. Now that dream suddenly seemed silly. Maybe it would be Shanetta's dream, not hers. The thought twisted her insides.

"Where we goin'?" she asked finally as Bluford disappeared in the distance.

"The beach," Cooper said. "Ain't been there since we took Darcy months ago, remember?"

Tarah closed her eyes and recalled the day last fall when they had gone there to complete an assignment for Ms. Reid's biology class. Tarah and Darcy weren't even friends then, but the teacher paired them up as lab partners. Cooper gave them a ride to the beach where they were supposed to be studying tidal pools. Darcy had seemed so snobby at first that Cooper started teasing her. Then, as a joke, he tossed a bug down Darcy's shirt. That's when Darcy went crazy.

"I remember Darcy kicking you," Tarah said picturing the whole event in her mind. It seemed like ages ago, though it had only been months. "I can't believe she stomped you. You asked for it, though."

"I can't believe it, neither. I still got a bruise from that day. It was like she was wearing spiked shoes or something!" he said, rubbing his leg as if it hurt.

Tarah smiled, and for a second everything almost seemed normal again. There was no painful secret she had hidden and

76

no Shanetta. It was just the two of them in the truck heading to the beach.

But as the miles rolled by, the doubts and memories crept back, and not even the noise of the roaring engine or the whooshing of wind could mask the awkward silence that grew between them. Tarah couldn't stand it.

"So where were you the other night?" she asked finally.

Cooper looked away from the road for a second. His eyes flashed with dark intensity. "I should ask you the same question." He switched lanes and took the exit toward Santa Monica State Beach. "Especially about this morning."

"Huh?"

"You ain't been yourself in days, Tarah. Weeks actually. I thought it was just me, but this stuff that happened this morning. You following up on me in school . . . I mean, I ain't never seen you like that."

Tarah shook her head. She wasn't ready for Cooper to start asking her questions, and she wasn't about to answer them. She wasn't the problem here. Cooper was the one sneaking around with Shanetta and hiding it from her.

"Whatchu know about this morning?

You talk to Shanetta already? So is it true? Are you seeing her? Is that what you came here to tell me?" Tarah couldn't hide the anger and hurt mixing in her voice.

Cooper winced. "See, there you go. That's what I'm talking about. You always thinkin' I'm up to no good."

"Yeah, but you didn't answer me. Maybe if you'd just answer my questions for once, we wouldn't be like this, okay?"

"Like what?" Cooper asked. He pulled the truck to a stop just a block from the beach. The afternoon sun hung over the ocean, glaring at them. "What are you trying to say? 'Cause if there's something I should know, you need to tell me, okay?"

Tarah shrugged, unsure how to respond. She knew he was right. Ever since she had heard about Uncle Rudy coming, she had changed. She had tried to hide it and pretend everything was normal, and maybe most people would be fooled. But not Cooper. She felt guilty for keeping the secret from him, but she didn't want him or anyone else to know about it.

"I ain't got nothing to say, okay? I'm not the one keeping secrets," she said, avoiding his gaze. "You the one doin' that."

Cooper sighed and yanked the keys from the ignition. Moments later they were walking on the beach. Waves crashed and died in the surf as they made their way closer to the water's edge. Normally, Tarah would have been thrilled to be out with Cooper, but now everything had gone wrong. It almost felt as if their relationship was like the waves breaking on the beach and then slowly slipping away.

"Look, Tarah, I don't know what's going on with you, okay? It's like you're someone else or you forgot who I am. I brought you here so I could remind you."

Cooper looked more serious than she had ever seen him. As she watched, he reached down and grabbed her hand. "It's true. I took Shanetta home, okay? But you got it all wrong. She likes Steve, not me. And like I told you before, I'm not interested in her. You hear me? Tell me you're listening."

A wave thundered in the distance as Cooper's words started to sink in. "*Steve?* So why you sneaking off in the middle of the night?"

79

"'Cause . . ." Cooper paused as if he was struggling with whether he should tell her. Then he shrugged, looking a little defeated. "'Cause he and Shanetta got into an accident."

"What?"

"You can't tell anyone this, okay?" Cooper insisted. Then he explained how guys from the football team had gathered at their teammate Clarence's house the other night. Steve was there.

"Shanetta been after him for days," Cooper said. "They were flirting all the time at practice, and we were teasing them. Anyway, he calls her and dares her to show up at this party. She did, but by the time she got there, people had been drinking. Some were getting high. Dumb stuff. Anyway, things got a little crazy. Someone musta said something to her, and she wasn't havin' it. She started yelling, and there was all this drama, so Steve went to take her home. But on the way, he clipped a pole with his car. They're lucky no one got hurt, but Steve's car got banged up."

Cooper's words made sense. They partly explained why Shanetta seemed so hurt at Bluford this morning. But what happened at the party to make her so upset? Tarah wondered. She felt a twinge of guilt for what she had said to the girl a few hours earlier.

"But that still don't explain how you got involved."

"Shanetta texted me. She had my number from that stupid picture she took. I was falling asleep and then I get this message that they're stuck. Neither of them wanted their parents to know, so . . . I just picked them up and took 'em home. Dude owes me big time 'cause I moved his car and got him outta there before the cops came. If they smelled beer or weed, they'da hauled his butt to jail. That woulda been the end of his football season. Maybe his scholarship chances, too."

"Why didn't you tell me this?" Tarah exclaimed, stunned at all this news. "Why you been hiding it?"

"'Cause Steve made me promise not to tell. 'Cause if anyone finds out, there's gonna be lots of trouble, and 'cause I thought no one would know. But I was wrong. Forgot about Dez asking where I was going when I left the house. Shoulda known he'd tell Jamee and that she'd start spreading gossip and Darcy would find out."

"She was only looking out for me."

"I know," Cooper said with a pained smile. "That's why I'm not too mad at her, but I'll tell you something. Next time Jamee goes spreading gossip that has nothing to do with her, I'ma put a bug down her back, just like her sister."

"Yeah, and she'll probably kick you too," Tarah said with a smile, feeling a wave of relief. "I can't believe you been hiding this from me. You didn't do nothing wrong. All you was tryin' to do was the right thing."

"But I shouldn'ta lied to you," Cooper insisted. "That's where the problems started. I told you when we got together that I would always be honest with you, and I mean it. My dad was never honest with my momma. He used to promise her he wasn't gonna drink no more, promise her that he would make everything better. But he lied over and over again. I never want to be him, okay? I want to be everything he wasn't. That's what keeps me going each day," he said, locking her in his gaze.

He rarely spoke about his father. It was his secret, something he revealed the first time they had gone to the beach together. He told her things that no one

82

else knew, things no one could see watching him swagger down the halls of Bluford High as if he didn't have a care in the world.

The truth was the opposite. That same night, he had confessed to how, when his father got drunk and started hitting, Cooper used his own body to protect his little brother and mother from the beatings.

"I knew if I could just hold tight, he'd get tired and walk away. And I had to do it 'cause if I didn't, what would happen to Dez or Mom?" he had said. *"But them bruises. They still hurt. They in here now."* He had pointed to his chest and head.

"You're nothing like him," she said, looking at him. "I know you won't never treat me like your daddy treated you. I can see it in your eyes," she told him. "I'm sorry I doubted you, Coop."

"But that's the thing, Tarah. I'ma say this, and you gotta stay quiet and hear me out. I know something's been eatin' at you. I know you're hiding things from me. I know there's something you don't want me to know. I can see it, 'cause I looked at my own momma for years with the same look."

Tarah felt her eyes moisten, and she

quickly blinked back tears, pulling them back inside the way the ocean reclaims its waves after throwing them at the beach.

"I can't make you talk, but I can't help you if I can't reach you. So I want you to know I'm here, baby. I ain't goin' nowhere. You are the best thing I got in this world right now, and I'ma do all I can to be there for you with whatever's happenin'. Y'hear me?"

Tarah gazed out at the beach and the waves. In the distance, a man walked a dog. Farther up, a little boy dug in the sand in front of two adults who watched him carefully. They were all people on the edge, on the tiny stretch where the land and the sea meet and fight each other. Tarah couldn't stop staring at them, even as her mind raced.

They were just four words. Four words that hung between them.

My uncle raped me.

But in those words was enough to tear worlds apart. They were words that ruined lives, that spawned unending nightmares and planted a lifetime of doubts, of insecurity, of pain and anxiety. Ugly words that pushed a permanent shadow into her life, and left an unwelcome ghost that stared back at her in every mirror, an accusing voice in even the quietest moments.

If I could just say the words, she thought to herself. *If I could just tell him.*

But the idea triggered endless questions that crashed through her mind like the waves before her.

What if he sees me differently after I tell him what happened?

What if he doesn't want to be with me anymore?

What if he sees me as ugly because of what Rudy did?

What if he walks away?

"I'm here," Cooper repeated, rubbing her back.

She nodded and closed her eyes, gently leaning into him.

"I know you are."

It was all she could say.

Chapter 7

"*What?* You're not going to the party?" Mom yelled, dropping the photo album she had been working on for days.

Tarah had rehearsed the conversation many times, but it didn't make Mom's outrage any less. Tarah had waited all day to find a quiet moment to talk to Mom. Aunt Lucille, Rochelle, and Kayla had finally left after spending hours preparing for the upcoming reunion. Tarah remained silent the whole time, waiting for them to leave so she could talk.

"It's Ms. Stephanie, from work," Tarah explained. "She needs me to babysit her son."

"Yeah, well, we need you at this reunion!" Mom exclaimed. "I can't believe I'm hearin' this. You knew this party was coming for months. Why all the sudden you gotta work now?"

"She's got a two-year-old, and she and her husband ain't been out in, like, forever. What was I gonna do?" Tarah said with a shrug, though she knew the answer.

"What were you gonna do?!" Mom hollered as if the question were an insult. "Tell her *no*—that's what you shoulda done. Let her find another babysitter that day."

"I can't, Momma. Ms. Stephanie's the one who says I should be a teacher. She's always complimenting me on my work, and I know she needs the help, so when she asked me, I said yes."

"Well, you shouldn't have!" Mom snapped. "This is Aunt Deborah's ninetieth birthday, Tarah. You should be celebrating with us. Lord knows we're not gonna have that many more birthdays with her," she added.

"I'm sorry, Momma, but I gotta work."

"Tarah Carson, I can't believe my ears right now. You're always dropping everything to help your friends when they need you, and now one time when your family needs you, you gonna say no?"

Tarah felt a stab of guilt. She knew

her mother was right, and she wanted to see Aunt Deborah too, but there was no way she could face Uncle Rudy again. Not even her love for her aunt could make her do that.

"I already told Ms. Stephanie that I'd do it, Momma. I can't just back out now."

"Just call her up. Tell her the truth. Tell her you got plans with your family. I'm sure she'd understand, Tarah."

"No!" Tarah blurted, surprised at how forceful her voice was. Her mother's eyebrows rose as if Tarah had just insulted her. "It's just that I made a promise to her, and I don't want to break it, not with all she's dealing with." Tarah hoped the words sounded convincing.

Mom eyed Tarah as if she was a puzzle that made no sense. Tarah struggled to keep calm as the seconds ticked by and her mother was silent. Finally, she spoke up.

"You're sixteen years old, so I'm not gonna make the decision for you. But you're making a mistake, and one day you'll regret it. You hear me?"

I know, Momma. But if you knew the truth, you'd understand why I can't go, she wanted to say.

Instead she shrugged and lowered her

eyes. She could see by the way her mother's teeth were clenched that she was furious. Whenever she got that way, Tarah knew the best thing she could do was to stay quiet.

"Forget that I might need you to help me set things up or that you knew about this party for months and coulda solved this whole mess by just telling Ms. Stephanie, or whoever, *no* the minute she asked you," Mom fumed, shaking her head. "Forget that Aunt Deborah is not in the best health. Forget all that." She shoved the photo album aside as if she were disgusted by what Tarah had said.

"No, the reason I am most upset with you is that you're gonna hurt her feelings. She's comin' out here all the way from Atlanta, looking forward to seeing you. This is the one day you can spend time with her, and you're gonna go and babysit some lady's child? That's no way to treat her. What kind of mother am I gonna look like with you not being there?"

"No one's gonna say anything about you, Momma. People gotta work some-times. Just tell them that."

"That's not the point, Tarah, and you know it!" Mom snapped, closing her eyes and shaking her head wearily. "Ever since you learned about this party, you been actin' strange. Rochelle said it too. Is there something else goin' on here? 'Cause I ain't ever seen you behave this way. It's like you're tryin' to find a reason *not* to be there."

Tarah squirmed in her seat. Her mother's piercing brown eyes suddenly made her feel cornered and trapped. She gazed at her own fingers and picked nervously at her nails, trying to pretend she couldn't feel her mother staring at her.

I'm sorry, Momma, she wanted to say. *I love Aunt Deborah too, but I can't be there, not with Uncle Rudy. Not again.*

There was no way she could admit the truth. Who would believe her? And even if they did, Tarah knew it would be like a bomb going off in her family, and she would be at the center. She would have to face each of them and admit how he had touched her and threatened her afterward.

"Don't you ever tell no one about this, you hear me? I'll hurt you if you do," he warned her that night, tugging her hair to emphasize his words. *"No one would believe you anyway."* Tarah had listened, hiding the truth ever since.

No one ever knew how scared she

had been that day. Today people said she was strong and funny, a loyal friend, someone who might be a teacher one day, like Ms. Stephanie said. If they knew the truth, Tarah figured, all that would change. They would see something else: a victim, someone to be pitied. Or worse, maybe they would see her as gross or filthy, the way the memories made her feel.

I can't have that, she thought as Mom watched her.

She knew how to stop it. All she had to do was wait for Rudy to go away again. Just a few days, and the party would be done, and he would return to Atlanta. She would have her life back, and nothing would change. Yes, it would hurt some people's feelings, and Tarah hated that, but it was the only way to keep herself together. It was the only way to stop Rudy from causing even more harm.

He already took my childhood, Momma. I ain't letting him take anything else, she thought. There was no way her mother or anyone else could understand, but it was better that way.

"That's not it, Momma," Tarah said. "I just gotta work, that's all. I promised Ms. Stephanie I'd help her, and that's what I gotta do, okay? But I'll try to get back so I can see Aunt Deborah before she leaves."

Tarah's mother sighed and shook her head. "This one's on you, Tarah. I don't like what you're doing here, and I'ma tell you something. If you can't be at this party, you better call Aunt Deborah and explain it to her yourself. That's the least you could do."

Tarah nodded, relieved that Mom didn't forbid her from working.

"I will, Momma," she replied as her mother grabbed the photo book and left her alone at the table. "I will."

All weekend, Tarah put off the phone call. All the while, her mother stressed over never-ending details: grocery lists, coolers and ice, supplies, transportation, tables, seating, and grills. Tarah stayed out of the way and ignored the conversations.

She babysat Kayla most of Saturday while her aunt and cousin took care of some last minute preparations, and on Sunday she spent the day with Darcy, who continued to obsess about Hakeem's return. Just the night before, Cooper told Tarah that he had spoken to Hakeem, and he had admitted he met a girl in

Detroit, someone named Anika.

"I don't think it's that serious, but he did stutter when he said her name," Cooper admitted. "He ain't stuttered to me in years."

"I'm not even tryin' to hear that right now," Tarah had said when Cooper told her. "Once Hak is back, they gonna be all right," she insisted, though she knew it was all just hope. "And don't go sayin' nothin' to Darcy about it neither. Ain't no use making her worry any more right now."

"So I guess we all keepin' secrets now, huh?" Cooper said, an edge to his voice.

Tarah ignored the comment. She knew what she had kept from Cooper was more than a little secret, and if she had to, she would take it to her grave without telling anyone what happened.

On Sunday night, after staring at the phone most of the afternoon, Tarah finally picked it up and nervously punched in Aunt Deborah's phone number.

"Auntie Deborah?" Tarah said as soon as she heard the shaky voice on the other end of the phone.

"Yes?" came the reply. The voice was scratchy, like sandpaper.

"It's Tarah, Clarice's daughter. How you doin'?"

"Tarah! Oh my goodness! So nice to hear from you," came the cheerful reply. Right away, Tarah cringed inside, knowing she was about to deliver bad news. For a few minutes they talked about Tarah's mother and Aunt Lucille, and how it had been too long since they had all gotten together.

"I can't wait to see you, Tarah," the old woman gushed. "I remember how you stayed with me almost the whole time at Aunt Linda's wedding. That was one hot afternoon, I'll tell you, but we made the best of it. You were just a little thing back then, so you probably don't remember."

"I remember some of it, Auntie," Tarah said, pacing in her room with the phone.

"It seems like only yesterday we were singing songs under that big old oak tree. You remember that?"

Dimly, Tarah recalled sitting beneath a giant tree on a blanket the color of mustard. Her aunt had been right next to her. Tarah stared in her bedroom mirror and squinted as the hazy memories trickled back to her.

"Kind of," Tarah said. Most of that day she had tried to forget, but now as Aunt Deborah described it, she could recall leaning back against her aunt and feeling her strong arms gently rocking her as she sang. "Why were we singing?"

"Best way to calm a child," Aunt Deborah said. "You were a little upset that day. I think the heat and all the strangers were getting to you. Lord knows, we got a big enough family," she added with a chuckle. "So we sat together, just you and me, like my grandmother used to do. We was singing old nursery rhymes. You liked 'Bah Bah Black Sheep' best. Then we sang some old hymns, too. You had the prettiest voice, babygirl! I told your momma back then we got to get you in the church choir. I hope you stuck with it."

Tarah smiled. She had watched some of the teachers singing to the little kids at Little Learning Spot, but she had not actually sung with them. Except for singing along to the occasional song on the radio, she hadn't sung in ages.

"It's been a while since I've sung, Auntie," Tarah confessed.

"Well, that's okay. You still got the songs inside you, right? You just waitin'

95

for the right time to sing 'em. Maybe we can sing a little when I see you. Only a few days now." Aunt Deborah coughed and then cleared her throat. "Of course my voice ain't what it used to be. You'll have to carry me this time."

Tarah felt a sinking feeling in her stomach. She knew what was next, the words that would disappoint her aunt. She wished she didn't have to say them, but there was no other way.

"That's why I'm calling, Auntie Deborah," Tarah said, taking a deep breath and then forcing the words out. "I got some bad news. I'm not gonna be at the party. I have to work."

The phone was silent for several seconds, and Tarah wondered if the call was dropped, but then the old woman spoke up.

"You mean you're not gonna be there at all?" she asked, her voice rising so that the last word was drawn out painfully. "You're one of the people I want to see the most."

"I'm gonna try and get there late, I swear, but I don't know if I'm gonna be able to make it. I gotta work," Tarah said, feeling horrible about what she had done. "That's why I wanted to talk to you."

Tarah didn't know what else to say. She didn't want her aunt to know that her mother was the reason she called. Yet the more they spoke, Tarah realized that Mom was right. She should have called.

"Well, I'll be honest, Tarah. I am a bit disappointed. I been looking forward to seeing you for months. I don't know how many more times I'ma make it out there. I'm getting old!" she said with a little laugh.

"I'm so sorry, Auntie."

"Don't be sorry. If you gotta work, that's what you gotta do. When I was young, you didn't walk away from a job, 'cause you never knew if you'd see it again, so I'm glad you're working. Besides, I think I'll be staying either at your house or Lucille's for a few days, so maybe you'll see me another day."

"For real? You're gonna stay here?"

"Yes, I'm flying out Thursday. Your Uncle Rudy's bringing me. We're travelin' together."

Tarah almost dropped the phone. For a second she couldn't speak. It was as if hands had suddenly gripped her throat.

"You there, Tarah?"

"Yeah, I'm here," Tarah said with a nervous gulp. "But I gotta go. So even if

I don't get to the party, I'll definitely see you. I'm glad it's gonna work out."

"Me too, babygirl. See you in a few more days."

Tarah said goodbye and hung up, her palms slick with sweat.

Chapter 8

"Momma, is Aunt Deborah really gonna be staying here?" Tarah asked later than night. Her mother was stretched out on the couch watching TV after cleaning the house all afternoon.

"Maybe. Lucille and your Uncle Carlton haven't figured out where everyone's gonna be. All I know is with all the people we got coming, somebody's gonna stay here. Why you askin'?"

"Whatchu mean *somebody?*" Tarah asked a little too forcefully.

"Whatchu think I mean? I mean *somebody*. Aunt Deborah, Rudy, Corbett, Aunt Gigi . . ." She listed several more relatives, but Tarah's mind snagged when she mentioned Rudy. It was something she had never considered.

Rudy staying overnight at their house.

Her stomach churned. "How come you never told me?!"

"Tarah, why do you think I been cleaning all day, huh? I been talking about it for weeks. I sat here with Rochelle and Lucille and planned everything the past two weekends. You were right here. Don't you remember?"

Tarah shook her head. She had done all she could to avoid the discussions about the party. Most of the time, when they were talking, Tarah played with Kayla or hid in her room.

"Just 'cause you weren't listening doesn't mean we didn't discuss it. We got a big family, so someone needs to stay here. You understand now? Besides, what difference does it make who's here?"

Tarah shook her head wearily. *All the difference, Momma,* she wanted to say. *Please don't bring him here.*

"Which reminds me, did you call Aunt Deborah and tell her you won't be at the party?" her mother asked.

"Yeah," Tarah said defensively, searching frantically for a way out, a way to avoid what now seemed inevitable.

"Good. Now another thing you gotta do is clean that room. It better be spotless while we got guests, okay?"

100

Tarah nodded. She wanted just to leave the house, jump in Cooper's truck, and drive away. Anywhere but home. But she knew that couldn't happen. No matter how hard she tried, there seemed to be no way to avoid Rudy. She couldn't imagine seeing him again in her own house after all these years. The thought made her queasy. There had to be something she could do.

"Tarah, you okay?" Mom asked, leaning forward from the sofa. She reached over and felt Tarah's forehead. Her hand felt warm as it touched Tarah's skin. "You look like you got a fever or something, but your temperature's fine. Your stomach bothering you again?"

"A little," Tarah mumbled, turning away from her.

"What is it, baby?"

Tarah felt desperate. For a second, she considered telling her mother the truth. But how could she do that now, just before the entire family arrived? Tarah imagined everyone staring at her knowing what happened, their eyes full of pity and maybe something worse. Maybe they wouldn't believe her. Or maybe some would get angry or blame her for hiding it for so long and using it to ruin the reunion. Just picturing it filled her with a wave of shame and made her want to hide in her room forever.

"I'm fine Momma, just tired, that's all. But I was thinking," Tarah said, grasping at the only thing she could think of to keep Rudy away. "Why can't Aunt Deborah be the one that stays with us? I spoke to her earlier, and since I can't get to the party, I thought maybe she could come here. That way I can see her. I'll sleep on the couch so she can have my bed."

Her mother nodded thoughtfully and rubbed Tarah's back. "Now that is the first good idea I've heard from you in a while. You know, I think if I say it like that to everyone, they'll probably agree with you. Aunt Deborah would too, I bet. But if she's gonna be staying in your room, I want it spotless. That means you need to be here to help me clean Friday night. Aunt Deborah always kept a spotless house, and if I'm having her here, we gonna make sure she feels at home, y'hear me?"

Tarah nodded in relief. At least she could keep Rudy away, off her sofa, and out of the little house they had lived in since she was in third grade—a place in which Rudy had never stepped foot. Tarah needed to keep it that way.

"You sure you feelin' all right?"

Tarah nodded and Mom leaned back on the couch. Tarah could feel her eyes scanning her, trying to figure out what was wrong.

"So what did Aunt Deb say to you when you talked?"

"She was telling me about the last time we got together. She said she sang me nursery rhymes back in the day," Tarah said.

"That's right! She did," Mom said with a big grin. "She had an amazing voice. Still does, actually. Sang in the church choir for many years with my grandmother."

"She's got a good memory, too. She even remembered the songs we sang."

"Mmm hmm," her mother agreed. "That woman's mind is like a steel trap. She can remember what she did fifty years ago. I can't even remember what I had for breakfast this morning," Mom added with a chuckle. "Well, I'm glad you spoke with her. I'm not happy you're missing this party. But at least you handled it well," she said, rubbing Tarah's back again. "My girl is growing up."

Tarah shrugged and tried her best to smile. She wished Mom hadn't praised her. She didn't feel as if she had done anything right. Instead, she felt guilty knowing the real reason for all of it—working, missing the party, calling Aunt Deborah—wasn't because she was doing the right thing. It was because she was scared and didn't know what else to do.

This time next week, they'll be gone. It'll all be over, she told herself over and over again.

Tarah had been repeating the words in her mind later that night when her cell phone started buzzing. She glanced at it and saw the text from Cooper.

U up?

She texted *yes*, and then he replied, asking her to call him.

"You ain't gonna believe this," Cooper answered on the first ring. "I just learned why Shanetta started fighting with Steve."

"What happened?"

"It was 'cause he lied to everyone about her."

"Whatchu mean?"

Cooper explained how one day after

football practice guys were in the locker room talking about Steve and Shanetta.

"Everyone was tryin' to see if he got with her."

"Why are they even askin' that? That's none of their business."

"C'mon, Tar, you know how it is," Cooper scoffed.

"That don't make it right, Coop."

"Who said anything about being right? This is locker room talk, Tarah. Anyway, Clarence joked about how they got busy, and Steve didn't deny it. He just smiled and laughed it off, and then everybody started asking details. I was just, like, 'Yeah whatever,' 'cause you know how that boy stretches the truth. But the thing is, when everyone was hanging out the other night, Shanetta found out he lied."

"Oh snap!" Tarah said, sitting up in her bed. "Are you serious?"

"So the night of the party, she put Steve on blast and started yelling at him, accusing him of lying. My girl went *off!* Made this big scene on the street outside Clarence's house. She actually slapped him when he was driving her home. That's why he swerved and clipped that pole. Now I know why she looked so upset when I got there. She didn't even look at me when I took her home. She still won't talk to anyone on the team. We used to see her every day. Not anymore."

Tarah felt a dull ache in her temples at the news. She had known for days that what she had said to Shanetta wasn't right. But Cooper's story made her words seem even worse.

"That's 'cause she's embarrassed," Tarah said knowingly. "People are making stuff up and making her look bad, and she can't do a thing about it. You know what people already say about her coming from 43rd Street and all that. I've said it too, but now I wish I hadn't. Steve better make this right."

"I don't know, Tarah. That dude's an idiot," Cooper grumbled. "He asked me to fix his car for him, and I said no. He made his own mess, and now he's gonna have to fix it himself."

Tarah nodded at his words. She knew she had some fixing to do, too.

"I actually thought you were better than that, Tarah . . ."

Shanetta's words echoed in her mind. Long ago, she decided the girl had a bad reputation. Since then she had ignored her and kept her distance. But the other

106

day, she realized Shanetta was sensitive to that charge. She cared what people thought about her. Now, thanks to Steve, her reputation was taking another hit. And it was all based on a dumb boy's lie.

Tarah knew she could let it go and ignore Shanetta. But if she did, Tarah was sure the girl would think she was just another person who believed Steve, another person who would accept a hurtful rumor, a person who would just go along with a lie.

That didn't feel right to Tarah. She was sick of lies. She had been living one in her family that was so deep and old, she didn't know how to fix it. But this one was new and easy to rip out. For the first time in a long time, she felt as if she could do something right, no matter what else was going on in her life.

"Anyway, I'm gettin' a headache talking about Steve. Enough about him. Whatchu doin' tomorrow?" he asked, yawning into the phone.

"I'ma talk with Shanetta," Tarah said.

"*What*?"

"Don't worry, Cooper," she said, feeling more certain than she had in weeks. "I got this."

* * *

The next morning, Tarah waited again outside Bluford for the dance team to complete their practice.

Shanetta spotted her the second she walked outside. Tarah could see the recognition in her face, the creases in her forehead as she scowled at her. Aisha and Monica were again at her side as she approached. Aisha crossed her arms as Tarah neared her.

"What you want *this* time?" Shanetta asked. "I told you, you got it all wrong, okay? Your head too *thick* to get that?"

"I got something to say to you, okay?" Tarah snapped back. "This time I'ma expect something better from you than stupid 'fat jokes,' y'hear me?"

Shanetta stopped in her tracks, as though what Tarah said surprised her. Then she rolled her eyes, put her hands on her hips, and sucked her teeth. "Whatchu want?"

Tarah took a deep breath. She knew what she had to say was right, but it didn't make it any easier. "I was wrong the other day," Tarah said. "And I'm sorry for what I said and for what that idiot Steve said. That boy ain't got no right to be talking about you, and I'ma make sure that I set the record straight if

I hear him sayin' any nonsense. That's all I got to say."

Shanetta's eyes opened wide, and she looked to each of her friends as if she was puzzled by what she had heard.

"Why you sayin' this to me? We ain't friends, and this really doesn't have anything to do with you."

"You're right," Tarah nodded. "I'm sayin' it 'cause it's the right thing to do. There is enough nonsense goin' on around here every day, and I don't want to be part of it. What I did the other day wasn't right, and when I heard what Steve did, I figured I should come to you straight up and set things right. That's all."

Tarah looked back toward the bus stop. Shanetta paused for a second. The scowl on her face was gone. Her two friends had stepped away and were texting on cell phones.

"There *is* a lot of nonsense around here. I'll give you that," Shanetta said with a shrug and a flicker of a smile. For a second, she seemed much younger. Tarah could almost see her as a child, like the kids she watched at the daycare center, not the swaggering girl at Bluford. But just as quickly it was gone, and the tough girl from 43rd Street returned.

"What I said about you the other day wasn't cool, neither. I guess I'm sorry, too," Shanetta said. Her eyes dropped then and she seemed to focus on a spot on the ground as if she didn't want to see Tarah looking back at her. "Except for my friends, you the only person to come up and say you don't believe all the rumors."

"Who cares what people think? They don't know nothin' anyway."

"You say that, but when school starts in a few weeks, everyone's gonna be talking. You know what they gonna say about me. You probably heard it yourself. One guy on the football team started talking to me yesterday 'cause he thinks it's true. He just wants to get with me 'cause he thinks I'm easy!"

"Why you even talkin' to him?" Tarah asked. "Look, not everyone's gonna believe what Steve said. Everyone knows his mouth runs faster than his feet. And the ones that believe him don't deserve to be near you, girl, so just brush 'em off and move on. Besides, me and Cooper got your back."

Shanetta glanced back at her friends. Tarah could see that they were waiting for her and starting to get impatient.

"I know you gotta go. Me too. My bus is comin'," Tarah said.

"Thanks for coming here, girl," Shanetta replied. "How you manage to get through each day without stuff driving you crazy? You always seem like you got it all together."

Tarah flinched inside, knowing just how stressed she had been over the past few weeks and how much she had struggled to keep her own secrets from swallowing her.

"Girl, I'm crazy, too!" Tarah said with a smile. "Maybe I just hide it well. I'll see you at school in a couple weeks. I gotta go to work now."

Tarah boarded the bus, feeling that craziness was brewing in her chest, especially with the reunion right around the corner.

"Just a few days, and it'll all be over," she repeated quietly to herself as her bus thundered through the city.

Chapter 9

"Make sure you scrub the kitchen floor, too," Mom shouted Friday night after supper.

"I *will*," Tarah yelled back. She was busy washing the dishes and trying to hide the nerves that erased her appetite and made her hands tremble. Her mother was down the hall cleaning the bathroom.

Suddenly, Tarah's phone started buzzing on the kitchen countertop. She glanced at the new text from Cooper.

U still havn bbq tmrw?

Tarah dried her hands on the kitchen towel and quickly texted him back that she was babysitting and would miss the party. Then she told him she wanted to see him Sunday.

"You clean your room yet?" Mom asked from the distance, interrupting her.

"Yeah, but I still gotta vacuum," she hollered back, putting the phone down. Just then, she heard knocking at the front door.

Tarah rushed over and looked through the tiny peephole to see her Aunt Lucille standing on the stoop, her black hair streaked with patches of silver. Tarah quickly opened the door and let her aunt in.

"Smells like some cleaning's going on in here," she said with a smile, placing a plastic bottle of detergent on the counter. "This is for your mother," she explained. "We doin' the same thing over at our place. If only I had you to help me instead of Rochelle, we'd be done right now. That girl could use a lesson or two in cleaning," Aunt Lucille complained.

"Thanks, Lulu," Mom said, stepping into the hallway for a minute. "So you all ready?"

"Just about," her aunt huffed. "Carlton picked up Aunt Deb and Rudy at the airport an hour ago. They're staying with him tonight. Tomorrow night after the party you got Aunt Deb, and Rudy'll

113

stay with me. I hope Rudy don't expect to sleep late. Kayla gets up at about 7:00," she said with a laugh. "Anyway, Denise is bringing an extra grill and Troy's bringing . . ."

Lucille listed a series of details, but Tarah had stopped listening. Her mind snagged on two words her aunt said earlier.

Rudy and *Kayla.*

The kitchen suddenly seemed to spin. Tarah's stomach felt as if it was sinking, as if her insides had instantly become hollow and everything was falling away somehow.

No. No. No! Tarah told herself as the meaning of Aunt Lucille's words started to seep into her mind like a poison.

Lucille had done just what she requested. Tarah had changed everyone's plans and got Aunt Deborah to stay at her house. But there was something in that arrangement she hadn't fully considered, a horrifying thought she had overlooked until this very moment.

Rudy would be near little Kayla.

That can't happen!

Tarah's mind spun with unspeakable

images of the sweet little girl enduring what had happened to her. Tarah knew that if it were to happen, it would be her fault for causing Rudy to stay there and never telling anyone else what he had done. She felt a sudden tightness in her throat, almost as if she couldn't breathe. Aunt Lucille was still talking, mentioning something about a final trip to the grocery store when Tarah cut her off.

"How you gonna fit Uncle Rudy in your house? You ain't got any more room than we do, and you got Kayla, too."

"He's gonna sleep on the couch. Where else would he sleep?"

"So Kayla and Rochelle are gonna stay together in her room?" Tarah asked. She knew it might seem strange for her to be asking, but she couldn't help herself. The questions boiled from within her.

"Yeah, like always. Why you askin' me? You got a better idea?"

"Nah," Tarah said with a shrug. "Just wondering how you gonna keep everybody comfortable, that's all."

Mom and Aunt Lucille exchanged glances but continued their conversation.

At least Rochelle and Kayla would be together, Tarah thought. Rudy wouldn't do anything with Kayla's mother and grandmother right there, she figured. Still, she couldn't shake the nagging feeling that Kayla wouldn't be safe anywhere near Rudy. He had hurt Tarah in her own bedroom when she was barely older than Kayla. The memory, stronger than ever, flashed in her mind. A dish slipped from her shaking fingers and clanged in the sink. She grabbed the counter for an instant to steady herself.

What if something happens to Kayla?

The question screamed in Tarah's mind over and over again as Mom and Aunt Lucille stepped into the living room to talk. No matter how she thought about it, Tarah felt responsible for Kayla. The little girl was her closest cousin and almost like her own child. She had changed her diapers and helped raise her since the day she was born. She had rushed her into the house several times over the years when gunshots rang out on nearby streets, covering her protectively with her own body.

The idea that she was going to put little Kayla in danger clashed against everything she lived for. Yes, she was scared of Rudy. That fear had led her to do all she could to avoid him. But that fear was nothing compared to Tarah's boundless love for Kayla and the fierce drive she felt to protect her.

The little girl would not be safe if she were left alone with Rudy. Tarah felt that with all her being. And with every cell in her body, from her skin right down to her bones, Tarah knew something else, too: she would not let Rudy harm Kayla.

Hours later, in her spotless room, Tarah stared at the ceiling with one thought repeating over and over in her mind like an endless prayer.

No matter what happens, please let me keep Kayla safe.

On Saturday, Tarah didn't want to leave for Ms. Stephanie's house at 2:00, but there was no escaping it. In trying to avoid one mess, Tarah had created an even bigger one.

Her mother had left for Municipal Park hours earlier to set up for the party, and Tarah had helped her, filling the trunk of her small sedan with bags of groceries, two rickety folding tables, a cooler of ice, and the beautiful photo book that Mom had finally finished for Aunt Deborah.

"I can't wait to see her look through

these." Mom had placed it on the passenger seat once the car was loaded. "You sure you're doing the right thing?" Mom had asked just before she left.

Tarah had nodded to her mother. But as she made her way to the bus stop, she felt as if everything she had done lately was wrong.

Lying to her mother.

Accusing Shanetta.

Doubting Cooper.

Avoiding the party.

Endangering Kayla.

A cloud of guilt hung over her as the bus rumbled over unfamiliar streets to Ms. Stephanie's two-story townhouse miles outside her neighborhood. She knew the only reason she was babysitting was because she had been scared. But she also knew she could not let that fear endanger Kayla.

As she stepped off the bus, Tarah knew her plan for the evening had changed. She could not avoid Uncle Rudy anymore. She would have to see him, she realized, in order to take Kayla away.

"Hi, Tarah," Ms. Stephanie said, as soon as Tarah rang the electronic doorbell. "I'm so thankful you could do this for us," she gushed.

A sweet fruity perfume filled the air, and Tarah could see her coworker was dressed in a nice skirt and a stylish, form-fitting shirt that made her look completely different than she did at work.

"You look so nice," Tarah said. "What would JJ say if he saw you now?"

Ms. Stephanie laughed and then introduced her husband. She quickly explained where everything was and what Drew's bedtime routine was. "We should be back by 7:30," she said. Moments later, they were off.

Tarah did her best to entertain the cranky toddler all afternoon and evening. But the whole time, her mind was on Kayla. Was Uncle Rudy talking to her? Was anyone watching him with her?

Tarah had Drew bathed and in his crib when Ms. Stephanie and her husband came back at 7:26. Tarah was in such a hurry she nearly forgot her pay as she rushed out the door.

"See you Monday," she said as she left.

It was almost 8:00 before Tarah finally arrived at Municipal Park. Her mouth was suddenly dry and her legs felt weak as she approached the park's main entrance. The low-hanging sun cast long shadows that stretched in gray bands along the street as she crossed it.

Even at this late hour, a number of familiar cars lined the park. Aunt Lucille's Focus. Uncle Carlton's beat-up Camry. Dozens of people stood around three still-smoldering grills. Tarah was sure some were relatives, though she only vaguely recognized their faces. Some of the men held soda cans or plastic cups and sipped them as they talked and poked at the fire. Along the side of the park, teenagers, including her cousins, were shooting baskets on the adjacent courts. Nearby, younger kids were playing what looked like tag between a row of trees. Laughter and a steady murmur of voices spilled into the park from a tall open tent the size of a small house.

From a distance, Tarah could see tables arranged in long lines like those in the Bluford cafeteria. The tables were still half full of people, some with plates and drinks in front of them. Occasionally a loud voice or the cackle of laughter boomed into the air.

"Now *that's* a party," said a middle-aged man to his companion. They were walking a dog along the edge of the park about ten yards ahead of her.

Tarah noticed many of the guests were dressed in yellow T-shirts. As she got closer, she could see that all the shirts were printed with the same words in blue lettering: "Jenkins Family Reunion" on the front and "Happy 90th Birthday, Aunt Deborah!" on the back.

Tarah eyed the tent to see if she could spot her mother or Aunt Deborah, but she didn't see them. Instead, she saw Aunt Lucille talking with some other women as they cleared an empty table. Just as Tarah reached the park, someone turned on music and an old hip hop beat kicked on. Laughter erupted as Uncle Carlton, standing near the grill, started dancing, doing some old school robotic move with a drink in his hand.

"Go Carlton! Go Carlton!" Aunt Renée, his wife, chanted. Normally, Tarah would have stopped to enjoy the spectacle of her uncle dancing, but not now. She had to find Kayla.

"Hey, Tar!" a voice called out. It was her sixteen-year-old cousin Troy. He was standing at one of the grills with a spatula in his hand. "You hungry?" he asked.

The other men at the grill turned, and suddenly a number of voices called out to her. She felt self-conscious in their gaze but kept walking forward, trying to stay as calm and natural as possible. All the while, her eyes scanned the crowd for Uncle Rudy and Kayla. She didn't see them anywhere.

"No, thanks," Tarah yelled back. "Troy, where's Kayla?"

"Rochelle took her home. She was getting tired. Been out here all day. I think she's gonna put her to bed now and come back."

"Come back?" Tarah repeated, her hands tingling at her sides. "Who's watching Kayla?"

"I don't know," Troy snapped. "Do I look like her babysitter? One of the uncles went back with her. Maybe he's gonna watch her."

"Who?" Tarah barked.

"I forget his name. Never met him before. Rufus or something."

"You mean Uncle Rudy?" Tarah asked, her pulse throbbing in her neck.

"Yeah, that's right."

Tarah bolted from the park, rushing down the street toward Aunt Lucille's house as fast as her feet could move her.

"Where you goin'? You didn't even eat!" Troy called out, but Tarah ignored him and the wave of nausea that threatened to sweep over her as she dashed down the street.

"You ain't touching that child," she declared with each step. "So help me, you ain't touchin' her."

The sunlight was fading as Tarah reached Aunt Lucille's house. Tarah grabbed the doorknob and twisted. It was unlocked, and in an instant she was standing in her aunt's living room. A rumpled brown suitcase was just inside the door. Though Tarah didn't see anyone, she could hear the sound of water running in the bathroom.

Where were they? She couldn't stop the images from flashing in her mind.

"Kayla? Rochelle?!" she called out, rushing down the hall, her limbs trembling.

"We're in here." Rochelle's voice came from Kayla's bedroom, at the end of the hallway.

Tarah rushed in to find Kayla lying on her bed in her favorite pink pajamas with a rainbow unicorn printed on her chest. Rochelle stood over her, tucking her into bed. Kayla's eyes were already half-closed, but she smiled sleepily when she saw Tarah.

"What are you doin' here?" Rochelle asked. "You should be at the party. It's winding down, but there's still people to see, and everybody wants to see you, too. Plus Uncle Carlton's chicken is so good!"

"I was there already. Uncle Rudy here?"

"Yeah. He's tired, though. Been out all day, plus the long flight. He's showering now and going to sleep. Not me! I'ma head back for a while. Kayla ain't gonna do anything but sleep anyway, so there's no point stayin' here. My girl is out," Rochelle said, nodding toward her daughter. Tarah could see that the little girl was already beginning to snore.

"So you just gonna leave?"

"Yeah. Why not? Uncle Rudy's here."

"You can't leave him here with her!" Tarah snapped.

"Why not?" Rochelle said, tilting her head as if confused by Tarah's reaction. "He's fine with it, Tarah. We talked about it. Besides, we're only a few blocks away. He's got my cell if anything happens."

In the distance, Tarah could hear the familiar metallic squeak of someone turning the water off. She knew Uncle

Rudy was about to get out of the shower.

"Don't leave her alone with him! He's a stranger to her."

"He's family, not a stranger," Rochelle snapped. "Besides, he can tell a story. Had me laughin' so hard, I had tears in my eyes."

Tarah shook her head in frustration. Rochelle didn't understand, and the only way she could convince her not to leave would be to tell her what happened. It was not something she wanted Rochelle to know, especially like this.

"So you just going to leave?"

"Yeah, once he's out of the shower. You should come with me. We won't be late, an hour or two at most."

Tarah grabbed her cell phone and quickly texted Cooper, her fingers shaking as she asked him to come to Rochelle's house right away.

"I'm not going with you, Rochelle," Tarah replied, feeling her phone vibrate an instant later. "I'm staying right here with Kayla." She glanced down at the screen to see Cooper's reply.

OK. On my way.

"Whatever," Rochelle huffed, rolling her eyes and stepping around her. She stopped in front of the closed bathroom door.

"Bye, Uncle Rudy," she called out. "Kayla's sleeping. I'ma go back before it gets too late. Thanks for watching her."

"Okay," said a muffled voice behind the door, sending icy threads into Tarah's veins. "See you later."

"Oh, by the way, Tarah's here too," she added before rushing out.

The front door shut with a heavy thud. Suddenly, the hallway grew close and silent. After all the years of fear and worry and pain, Tarah found herself alone again with Rudy.

Chapter 10

Tarah's heart felt as if it was about to burst from her chest. But fear couldn't move her from the hallway in front of Kayla's door.

Despite the trembling in her legs and the racing of her heart, she also felt a protective fury in her bones, anchoring her feet to the ground as if they were tree roots. She would not leave Kayla alone with him, not as long as she had strength in her body. Even if her mother did not or could not understand, Tarah would not let anything happen to the sleeping child.

The bathroom door opened, and a man—not the teenager she remembered —stood before her in shorts and a white T-shirt. He was no taller than her now, and his shoulders were slouched and soft looking. He had a slightly receding hairline, and his rounded stomach was nothing like the wiry person that had crept in her room a decade ago. But the eyes, the glassy black almonds that stared back at her, were the same. And in them, she could see recognition.

"I remember what you did to me," Tarah growled, clenching her hands into fists. "You ain't gonna hurt her the way you hurt me. Y'hear me?"

Uncle Rudy looked around the hallway warily as if to see who was listening. For an instant, the hall was silent. "I don't know what you're talking about," he replied quickly, his breath smelling distinctly of beer.

"Don't you lie!" Tarah hissed. Years of anger and hurt and rage drove her forward, and she shoved him away from Kayla's doorway. The force knocked him back against the wall with a thud. His eyes widened in surprise as he scrambled to keep his balance.

"I ain't never said nothin' to nobody, but I remember. You stole my childhood that night. I was just a little girl, and you took it. Y'hear me?!" Tarah fumed, fury and pain spilling into her voice. "I ain't never been the same, carrying this around all these years when the one

128

who should be carrying it is *you*."

Her uncle winced at her words. "Tarah, I was fifteen. I . . . I'd been drinking—"

"Don't even try to excuse what happened!" Tarah snapped. "There ain't *no* excuse for what you did!"

"Look Tarah, you can't tell anyone about this," her uncle pleaded. "I'm engaged. All that's behind me."

"What about me?!" Tarah boomed. "It never ends for me!" Tarah heard stirring in Kayla's room. She lowered her voice into a growl. "And why you here alone with my little cousin? Huh?"

The man's eyes shifted, as if he had gotten caught in a lie. "No, you got it all wrong. It's not like that. I mean I wasn't gonna hurt her. Not like that—"

"Get out!" Tarah barked, shoving him again. "Go tell everyone what you did. They still there waiting for you."

"No!" he cried. "No one can know about this. They wouldn't believe you anyway—"

"Get out!" Tarah roared. "You're a monster in this family, and you don't belong in this house!"

"Calm down—"

"I said *get out!* I never wanna see you

again!" Tarah hollered, pushing him again and again until he was out of the hallway.

"You better not tell—"

"Get out!!!"

Rudy cursed and rushed out the door. Tarah quickly locked it and then felt her stomach begin to heave. She had just reached the bathroom when she began to retch and vomit and weep.

Long minutes passed before she heard a gentle tapping at the door.

"Aunt Tarah?" It was Kayla's voice still scratchy from sleep.

"Coming, baby," Tarah said, quickly washing her face and opening the door.

Kayla stood in her pajamas, her eyes squinting against the bright hallway light. "I heard noises."

"I know, but it's okay," Tarah assured her, taking her into her arms and sitting her on the couch in the living room. "We're gonna do something special tonight. A sleepover at my house, okay? Just us girls. That'll be fun, right?"

The little girl smiled and nodded, still half-asleep. Cooper arrived minutes later. Tarah met him at the door carrying Kayla in her arms, signaling for him to be quiet.

"We need to take her to my house.

We'll talk tomorrow, okay, Coop?" she whispered to him, realizing for the first time that she wantcd to tell him the truth. "I'll explain everything then."

Cooper was wide-eyed, and he looked worried, but he also nodded as if he understood her. He didn't ask a single question as they took the short drive back to her house. She thanked him and even kissed his cheek before saying goodnight and taking Kayla inside. She then made a snug bed for Kayla on the living room sofa.

Kayla sleeping at my house. I'll bring her back tmrw. Have fun.

She sent the text to Rochelle and then sat motionless in the quiet living room, listening to the gentle hush of Kayla's breathing. A stack of pictures rejected from Aunt Deborah's photo album were arranged in a neat pile on the coffee table. Tarah was sure that Mom left them there to show her aunt when she got in. She grabbed them and leafed through them, seeing her own unhappy face from years ago.

But there was one of her sitting on Aunt Deborah's lap. The image was blurry and out of focus, almost as if it had been taken through tears. But Tarah could tell that she was singing in it, singing a nursery rhyme with her aunt, despite the horror she had endured only hours earlier.

And suddenly, in the dark room, Tarah found herself humming a gentle tune to her baby cousin, a sleeping angel for whom she had faced her deepest fears to protect. The love in her heart, she realized, was stronger than any fear, no matter how old or how dark or how deep.

Aunt Deborah and Mom arrived less than an hour later. Tarah was still awake guarding Kayla when she heard their voices outside.

"Tarah?" Aunt Deborah called out as soon as she saw her. "Oh my goodness, look at you, child! You're all grown up!"

The old woman embraced her then. Though Aunt Deborah had just turned ninety, Tarah could still feel strength in her wiry muscles when they hugged.

"Oh, I missed you, child," her aunt said.

"I missed you, too, Auntie," Tarah replied and squeezed her back. She felt a sudden stinging in her eyes and quickly blinked back the tears that tried to gather in them.

"I'm sorry I missed your party, but I'm so happy you're here."

"And I'm happy to be here, child," the old woman said, touching Tarah's cheek.

"Tarah? Why is Kayla here?" Mom asked from behind her. "Rudy said you were gonna watch her over at Rochelle's. I thought he looked confused when he said it."

"Nah, I decided to bring her here," Tarah said, wiping her eyes quickly. "We're having a slumber party. Girls only."

Aunt Deborah looked once at the sleeping child and then closely at Tarah. "Well, you got the slumber part right. Not much of a party though, is it?" she said with a smile.

"It's about all the party I am up for right now," Tarah said, smiling back at her. "I did sing to her a little bit. Just like us in this picture."

"Oh yeah?" Aunt Deborah smiled and squinted to get a good look at the picture. "Look how much you two look alike."

"It's true," Mom added. "Even in the blurry picture, you almost look like sisters."

Tarah stared at the old photo, remembering the horror that could have happened if she had not rushed home.

And then a thought hit her, one that had never occurred to her before: If she had not suffered, she would never have gone over to Aunt Lucille's house. Instead, she would have left Kayla alone with Rudy, just as Rochelle did. The thought made her shudder.

"Tarah, are you all right?" Aunt Deborah asked, eyeing her carefully.

Tarah closed her eyes and nodded wearily. "I am now," she said.

"Whatchu mean *now?*" Mom asked. "Is it your stomach again? Should I take you to the doctor, baby?"

Tarah shrugged and wiped her eyes. She grabbed the picture of herself with Aunt Deborah. She saw a child there, one weighed down by the most horrible event she could imagine. And yet amidst it all, she was still singing. She could almost hear her kid voice rising from the safety of her aunt's lap. It was incredible to think that a child could endure so much and still live on.

And yet she had done it, she realized. She was a survivor.

In a way, she had been doing that ever since, rising up amidst the wounds and scars to be a protector, a guardian of children. Perhaps that's why some called her a teacher or sought her when they needed advice. Such things didn't take her pain away, but they allowed her to transform the hurt into something positive and good and beautiful. And that made the pain bearable, a kind of antidote to the poison left inside her.

Tarah had never understood the connection before, in part because she had kept it hidden. But now after everything that happened—and with Mom and Aunt Deborah at her side—she was tired of hiding.

"It's a long story, Mom."

"We ain't going anywhere," Mom answered. Aunt Deborah rubbed Tarah's back.

Tarah looked them in the eyes and could see the fierce love and concern both women had for her. She could feel it radiating like heat through the quiet living room, thawing her insides. There was a song in her heart, a sad truth she had held for so long. It was time to let it out.

"I think you're gonna want to sit down," she said, closing her eyes. "This isn't gonna be easy to hear . . ."

The next day, Tarah asked Cooper to drive her back to the beach. She didn't tell him that Uncle Rudy had taken an early flight back to Atlanta, or that her mother was going to speak with a prosecutor friend about how best to pursue him, or that she stayed up with Mom and Aunt Deborah most of the night hugging and crying and reminiscing.

Instead, she grabbed a cooler of soda, leftovers from the party, and a blanket so they could sit down together alone on the beach.

She spent the drive talking about Hakeem's return in a few weeks and the coming school year. Yet Tarah knew Cooper was smart enough to figure out she had something more important to say, though he didn't once hassle her with questions or demand that she talk. Instead, he was respecting her silence and giving her space until she was ready.

Again they strolled on the edge of the water, the crashing waves muffling all the other sounds, making them feel that they were alone together, the only ones on the edge of the earth.

"Cooper, this ain't easy for me," she finally began, squeezing his hand for a second before pulling away. "I never wanted you to know 'cause I was afraid you wouldn't wanna be with me no more. I was afraid you'd be disgusted, that you'd want to walk away."

"Girl, nothin' you gonna say would make me do that. You gotta understand that by now."

"Listen to me, Coop. Don't say that until you know, 'cause I can't have you lying to me, not about this."

"About what, Tarah? What is it?" he asked, his voice urgent with concern.

Tarah looked at the waves crashing down in front of them and heard the steady rolling of the surf. Against it she felt tiny, like a little girl again, before her uncle had come along and shattered her world. It was as though she was trying to reclaim that time, to go back and mend the broken pieces that had been left behind.

A tear rolled down her face. Normally, she would pretend it was the salt air, the bright sun, a bit of sand in her eye. This time, Tarah locked Cooper in her gaze, stepped close, and held both his hands in hers.

There was no more hiding. No more lying. No more jokes to distract him. The words rose like a tide inside her, and she let them spill.

"I was raped, Coop," she said, staring

down at the sand. "I was six. He was my uncle . . ."

She felt Cooper's strong legs buckle, felt the horrible truth sinking into his body, felt him shudder in disbelief and outrage. But she also felt him embrace her, and when she tasted salt water on her lips, it wasn't the ocean. It was his tears mixing with hers.

Around them, waves crashed. Gulls cried. The sun inched across the sky. But for a long time, all Tarah felt was Cooper's arms.

"We gonna get through this together," he said finally. "I promise you that. This is only gonna make us stronger. Y'hear me?"

Tarah nodded, burying her face deep into his chest and hearing his heart beat, like the drum to a beautiful, perfect song.

"I know we will," she said, reaching for his hand. "I know we will."